praise for

medium normal ingrid

"Like the best ghost stories, Medium Normal Ingrid has wickedness, scares, courage, a mystery that lies beyond the grave, even young love. Like only a few ghost stories, it's filled with a love of language, an eloquence you will remember long after the story's graves are closed and its hearts have healed. Beautifully written."

–*David L. Robbins,*
NY Times best-selling author of *The Low Bird*

"A truly outstanding ghost story filled with mystery, intrigue, and questions that haunt us all.–Highly Commended."

Susan Keefe–TheColumbiaReview.com

I hope you enjoy!

medium normal ingrid

Wᵐ S. Tate

~~william s. tate~~

Little Star ✷

Published by Little Star

Richmond, VA

www.williamstate.com

ISBN 978-1-7323915-6-7

LCCN 2019913604

E-book: ISBN 978-1-7323915-9-8

Cover and interior design by Wendy Daniel.

Printed in the United States of America

For Alletta

chapter one

There's at least one too many people in my therapist's office. Dr. Spangler's writing on her pad, and I'm fidgeting with my locket while we wait for Dad. The Witch studies her nails. She's trying to give off a furious vibe, but she reeks of gloating. This emergency family session was her idea.

The laptop flickers, and Dad appears on-screen. His movements are palsied from the connection. The ocean glitters behind him. Our sky is fading to gray, but it's tomorrow morning and sunny in Dad's world. "I hate to be difficult," he says, "but I don't have a lot of time."

"Understood," says Dr. Spangler.

"Let's start with Ingrid's side of the story."

I pick a small truth to begin. "GC's a friend of mine—"

"You don't even know his last name," the Witch says.

"He needed a place to stay."

"Your bed?"

"It wasn't like that." My hands clench.

"I should've called the police."

"He didn't do anything."

The Witch scoots to the edge of her seat and raises a

william s. tate

finger. "Sneaking around with grounded teenage girls." She unfolds another finger. "Fighting." And a third. "Trespassing."

Dad's too pixelated for me to read his reaction.

"God knows what he was on."

I shake my head.

"We're here to talk about Ingrid," Dr. Spangler says, "and all of her tests have come back clean."

The Witch sits back. "She's out of control."

Dr. Spangler takes in my puffy eyes, and I crush an imaginary cyanide tablet between my molars. "How are you doing on your makeup work?" she asks.

"I still have three weeks."

"You've had all summer," says the Witch.

"I have one history paper left."

"Does she tell you," the Witch says, "that some nights she doesn't come home at all?"

"What Ingrid and I discuss—"

"I can't be responsible for her."

Dr. Spangler keeps her cool, "As I was saying—"

"She needs to be institutionalized."

"Tammie," Dad says.

"Can't you put her on lithium or something?"

I open my mouth to protest, but Dr. Spangler beats me to it. "I believe our best course of action," she says to the Witch, "is to continue to help Ingrid work through the grief associated with her mother's death and the nightmares resulting from the traumatic nature of the event. And in consideration of her mother's medical history, we will monitor her carefully throughout the process. But, as we have discussed, I see no need for chemical treatment at this time, and I have recommended no level of observation requiring institutionalization."

I want to hug her.

"There are plenty of doctors in this city."

"Can we all agree," Dad intervenes, "that the most important thing in the near term is for Ingrid to focus on her schoolwork?" Not even the Witch objects. "And it sounds like you two need a break from one another." I envy his control. "So let's find a scenario where Ingrid can get her work done and you two can spend some time apart."

"I could stay at the beach house," I say.

The Witch huffs.

Dad says, "How about a visit to your grandparents?"

I hear "the farm" but Dad means their new place. My gut clenches at the stupidity of giving up two hundred gorgeous acres for some dump in some backwater village.

The Witch shows her teeth.

And then it's the next day, and I'm on a train.

We shush to a stop at the platform where Grandma stands with the heels of her pumps touching, elbows in, hands clasped. Behind her a sign reads "Welcome to the Historic Village of Warwick," hand-lettered in dignified blue and gold.

Her hug is bony and cautious, like she's afraid one of us will break. She asks why I'm carrying a twig of a maple tree in a paper bag. "I dug it out of the yard."

"Just like your mother," Grandma says. I tell myself she means this as a compliment.

On the drive to their new place, she asks how things are going. By which I guess she means either my therapy or getting back into school or my war with the Witch. "Fine," I say. "Thanks."

We cross a commercial district with shops and municipal-looking buildings around a central park. Then we're passing Victorian houses with fancy porches and lace curtains and purple asters in tidy beds. The whole thing's vaguely museum-ish, like an elaborate diorama. On the other side of the road, an iron fence separates us from the grassy hills piling up and away to mountains, their peaks afire in the setting sun. Mom would stop the car for this.

"Your father sent me an email." Grandma says. She almost never says his name. "He asks how your history paper is coming."

"Tell him to tell the Witch to give my phone back. He can ask me himself."

"I'd like to give him a good report."

"So would I." I see Dad in some skyscraper in Singapore,

oblivious to the glistening sea. I wonder if Mom's ashes have drifted that far. "Do you think it's possible," I say, "if two people think about each other at the same time, would they feel it?"

Grandma touches my arm. "He'll be home soon, I'm sure."

But I'm not talking about Dad. "What if someone was thinking about me, and I was thinking about them at the same time, and our thoughts connected somehow?"

"If you want to call him ... "

"Remember in *Jane Eyre*, when St. John proposes to her?" A stone bridge appears ahead of us. "But she loves Rochester, and even though he's back at Thornfield, she hears him calling her name."

"You're not hearing voices," Grandma asks, "are you?" She disguises her worry with a laugh.

I could open the door, fling myself out. "I'm talking about love so intense it can cross time and space."

"I believe your doctor advised against romantic entanglements for now." Her tone is serious. "Your mother started with voices."

As if I didn't know.

"What can we do to help you?"

She could swerve off the bridge. "Maybe you could stop browbeating me about a stupid history paper."

"Your father wants you to focus."

I could enlighten her to the fact that Dad wants me

back in boarding school so I won't bother the Witch. But Dr. Spangler's in my head, reminding me not to perpetuate the negativity, so I keep my mouth shut.

We stop in front of another Victorian house, but this one's three stories of flaking shingles held together by vines and scaffolding. There's a tree growing out of a gutter. I'm seriously hoping we've run out of gas, but no, Grandma says we're home.

Grandpa's out front talking to a couple of guys by a pickup truck. He waves and comes over as they drive off. His hug is strong and warm, and he smells of sandalwood. "What do you think?" A shutter hangs on one hinge, exposing a shadow of less-faded paint.

"You sold the farm for this?"

"Needs some work." He looks at Grandma, who squeezes out a smile on her way up the porch steps. "But it's got good bones." Grandpa takes my suitcase. The porch sags as I follow them inside.

"If you need a break from your schoolwork," he says. "I'd love your help with the garden."

"Is that what you call it?" My tone's too sharp.

Grandpa takes my maple seedling. "Izzy would be proud." Only Grandpa ever got away with calling Mom Izzy.

"It's for my room."

"Speaking of which," Grandma says, and we navigate a labyrinth of plastic sheeting and moving boxes. We climb to the third floor, which consists of a bathroom and an undersized door that creaks when she opens it.

"It used to be the maid's room," Grandma says.

The space is narrow and tall and smells like mice. Rough-paneled walls angle inward at waist height. Rafters criss-cross the narrowing space. At least there's a window, a dormer, just wide enough to stand in.

Grandma clicks a chain. A bare bulb glares, and shadows swing to life.

A girl whispers in my ear, quiet but urgent. *Help me.* I startle and turn to the voice, but it's only Grandma and me. I stifle my panic.

She gives me a scrunched look. "I know it's not ideal, but it's the best we could do on short notice."

"I'm sorry," I say, not really sure why I'm apologizing.

"Of course we're thrilled you're here. I wish the house were—"

"No," I stop her. "It's great to be here, really. I'm just tired. From the trip." And from not sleeping through a night since Mom died.

"I'm afraid the workers start very early, but they promise they'll be done in a few weeks."

"It's fine," I say, just wishing I could be alone.

And then I am.

The furniture isn't from the farm, but it's old. There's a tiny bed and a dresser with drawers that smell like dried glue. There's an alarm clock with real bells. I wind it and set it, and I like how it ticks. A child-sized desk holds a lamp, and there's a framed photograph of Mom and Dad I've never seen. The light from the flash makes them pale and sparkles off Mom's locket, the one around my neck now. I toss the picture into a drawer and cringe as the glass shatters.

In the locket is a picture of me cannonballing off the pier. Dad said I should replace it with one of Mom, but I don't need to be reminded of her. I'd rather remember me, the girl I was when she was alive. In the locket she's still there, along with the razor I carry, just in case.

A breeze sweeps through the window and sets the bare bulb swinging again. The light winks off the glass. Something flickers in my peripheral, and I hear the girl again. *Help me.*

"Grandma?" I say to no one. My heart's galloping, and the back of my neck's bristling as I step into the empty hall, check the empty bathroom. A drop of water hangs on the spigot then plunks into the drain. I glance into the empty staircase. "Mom?"

It could've been anything: tree branches rubbing, an echo from the pipes, an animal in the walls. I tell myself it was some perfectly ordinary, old-house noise, and I try not to think about mice nosing around in the dark, and I tell myself please don't dream.

I gasp awake for the hundredth time, panting from a battle against something: tentacles, hands, my sheets, soaked and twisted around me, dragging me down, down. My alarm's about to go off, and once again I feel more exhausted than I was when I went to bed. I lay there until the alarm, then I get up, brush my teeth, battle my pimples, brush my hair. By the time I'm dressed my sheets are dry enough to pull taut around the mattress. Routine's important, according to Dr. Spangler, a controlled dose of O.C.D. to inoculate me against something worse.

In the kitchen, Grandpa's reading a newspaper and sharpening his gardening shears. Grandma pushes a copy of *House Beautiful* over a photocopied article from *The Journal of Clinical Psychiatry*, the April issue, on dopamines and schizophrenia.

"I've read that one," I mumble. "My PET scans are fine."

"You don't look well," Grandma says. "Did you sleep at all?"

"Is there another room I can use?"

"You'll have to get used to the third floor," Grandma says.

"It's creepy up there."

"It'll be plenty nice," Grandpa says, "when the renovation's done."

I open cabinets to find a mug. "If I survive that long."

Grandma and Grandpa go silent at this, so I clarify. "It's just an expression." I bang the cabinet too hard.

"I wish you wouldn't—" Grandma starts.

"I wish you wouldn't over-analyze everything I say." I find a mug and pour the dregs of the coffee.

"We can't ignore those types of comments," Grandma says. "Not in your state."

"My 'state' is that I'm fine." The coffee's sludge, and I spit it into the sink. "I'm just tired."

"Do you think you'll begin your schoolwork today?" Grandma asks.

"I don't know." I find the coffee can to reload the maker.

Grandma says, "it's important for someone in your condition—"

"I don't have a 'condition'?"

"You've suffered a horrific event."

"Thanks for reminding me." Of course the can is empty.

"It's nothing to be ashamed of."

I want very badly for her to shut up. "Who said I was ashamed?"

"You're obviously angry."

I slam the can into the trash. "Why would I be angry?"

"Sarcasm won't help. Dr. Spangler says—"

"She talked to you, too?"

"Only to say that you're making progress with your issues."

"My 'issues'?"

"It's perfectly normal."

"Perfectly normal girls don't have 'issues.'"

"Listen to yourself. You're—"

"I'm fine," I say on my way outside.

"Where are you going?"

Not that it's any of her business, but out of courtesy I yell, "for a walk," as I pound down the front steps. I speed past the two worker guys hauling tools out of their pickup and turn down the road to follow the spiked, iron fence in the direction of the commercial district.

I didn't notice yesterday, but headstones and crypts dot the hills behind the iron fence. Way off rises the spire of a pyramid that's taller than any grave marker I've ever seen. I ask myself how I missed that before and what else I haven't noticed. I also wonder where I'm going.

Another of Dr. Spangler's requirements is that I write in my journal every day. She says careful observation and self-analysis are important after what she calls a deep emotional trauma. A side effect of this is that I often find myself narrating my own life as I think about my next journal entry. So as I walk I'm describing last night's nightmares, forcing myself to believe that the woman isn't really Mom, that she's not really in my head, that she's not trying to torture me into killing myself. Instead it's like Dr. Spangler says, it's just my subconscious processing her suicide. I can believe the nightmares are just my imagination, but that voice begging me for help was something else. If it's a hallucination, I'm doomed. There has to be an explanation, so I'll just move forward with Dr. Spangler's plan while I figure it out. Dr. Spangler says if I stick with the plan, life will be normal again one day. "That's where I'm going," I say aloud. I'm going to be normal.

I cross the stone bridge and enter an old-fashioned town square with cobbled streets and brick sidewalks and wide-windowed storefronts. There's a grassy central park and a bandstand.

There's nothing really wrong with the scene, but something isn't right. It takes me a few minutes to put my finger on it, but it's too clean: no litter, no graffiti, no hot-garbage smell of the city. The camphor of geraniums accents the air. The only unclean thing about it is the mousy, attic smell clinging to me. Even the drone of a lawnmower— it must have been there all along—only highlights the immaculate calm of the place.

My reflection warps and bulges across the storefront windows, floating on the cloudless sky behind me. In the square, pockets of haze hover in the shadows of trees. I cross the grass toward the Town Hall at the far end of the square.

On a rise beyond the Town Hall looms a stone mansion, solid and still as the mountains that ring the horizon. A guy, maybe my age, is pushing a mower in front of the mansion.

The buzzing engine feels like the only tether connecting the Historic Village of Warwick to the twenty-first century.

In a window on the top floor of the mansion, a woman, maybe a girl, pushes aside a curtain to look out.

I'm pondering why anyone who could afford a house like that would live in this forgotten village when the mower stops. In the flood of silence, the guy notices me and starts to come over. The third floor curtain falls closed.

The guy tracks through the wet grass in his cargo shorts. A ring through his eyebrow flashes in the sun. He keeps coming like he's going to run me over and finally stops so close that I'm enveloped in the tang of gasoline and cut grass and sweat.

His bangs stick to his forehead in brown angles. His brown eyes blink. His cheeks soften into a smile, undermining whatever affect he's going for with the piercing. He's not handsome, but cute. Possibly aphasic. Not afraid to stare.

"You don't look like an Ingrid," he says, dispelling the aphasia theory.

"Who are you?"

"Burt."

"How do you know my name, Burt?"

"Your grandfather."

I pretend I don't care. "What else did he tell you?"

"He didn't tell me you looked like this."

The way he hits the word "this" makes me wish I'd

showered, and I wonder how many Warwick girls have insomniac eyes and hair the color of clover.

"Did you see Mrs. Stirling yet?" he asks.

I don't know this name, and I shake my head, wondering what I've missed.

"Judge Stirling saw her all the time."

"I don't know what you're talking about."

"Dorothy Stirling's ghost."

A laugh snorts out before I can stop myself, but he keeps going. "Warwick's the third most haunted town in the country."

Instinct says to flee, but I stay put. "Do I look like somebody who believes in ghosts?"

He studies me for a moment. "What do you think happens, then? When you die?"

I blink out of his gaze. Insects hover over the grass he's just mowed. A bird hops among them, picking them off. I know this one.

"Do you think you just—"

"First," I cross my arms, "it goes dark—"

Burt raises his ornamented eyebrow.

"—and the engine pumps out carbon monoxide. It attaches to your hemoglobin, and you turn pink as you asphyxiate." I uncross my arms. "Your daughter finds you and cries and screams at the nine-one-one guy, but you just lay there until the firemen cover your face with a mask and load you into the ambulance. You disappear into the hospital. Then the incinerator. Then you're smoke and ashes." And nightmares.

Burt's mouth opens.

"Anything else, Burt?"

"Yeah." He's nodding. "I could show you around if you want."

"No, thanks," I turn and start walking.

"At least tell me what it's like," he says to my back.

"What what's like?"

"Living in a haunted house."

chapter two

I'm walking away from Burt, pretending he didn't just say "haunted house." But he did, so he's either a weirdo or he's trying to be funny. But he talked to Grandpa, so maybe he knows about Mom. So if he thinks that's funny he has a shitty sense of humor.

It feels like he's still watching me, but finally the mower roars back to life. Dr. Spangler's in my head reminding me to give him the benefit of the doubt, telling me I need to open up more, to make friends. And I'm thinking that wasn't a very good way to go about it and maybe I should've been more polite. Maybe I should have accepted his offer.

Grandma's car yelps to a stop beside me. Her phone's to her ear, and the window's coming down. Her eyes narrow into a face that says she's relieved but not pleased.

She ends her call. "You had us worried sick." Not at all friendly.

"I'm sixteen."

"Which is old enough to demonstrate common courtesy."

"I said I was going out."

"I'd appreciate it if you would be a bit more specific in the future. You're our responsibility for the next three weeks. Please get in."

"Why don't you just track my phone?" I drop into the passenger's seat and slam the door. "Oh, right," I say. "No phone."

I pass the afternoon alone in my room, watching the glaring light soften to dusk. Grandma demands my presence at dinner and annoys me with questions, then I'm back upstairs, alone with the cooling sky and the stirring trees. My history paper isn't writing itself. I don't want to think about history, and somehow it's dark now. So I tell myself a good night's sleep's what I need, that tomorrow I'll rise anew, start my paper and continue down the path to normal.

I click on the bare bulb and sit for a minute in its swaying glow and the chorus of insects. My maple's lost another leaf. I balance my journal against my legs to compose the prescribed entry.

In tiny cursive I describe my encounter with creepy, cute Burt, and how he actually asked me if I'd seen a ghost, and he called her by name—Dorothy Stirling—and by the time I've analyzed and re-analyzed the scene, I'm fully regretting my monologue. I find myself waxing about his dimples, and his grassy, sweaty scent that should have been gross but, on recollection, stirs something pleasant in my stomach, and I'm believing his talk of ghosts and haunted houses weren't sociopathic warnings but misguided attempts at flirtation, and how I ought to be nicer in general. I owe him an apology. Grandma, too.

I consider mentioning what I heard last night, but I can't think of a way to write it down that doesn't sound like a symptom. Admitting I heard a disembodied voice would be Exhibit A in the Witch's case for institutionalizing me. Instead, I explore my motives for wanting to apologize to Burt. Am I looking for a boyfriend? Any friend? Someone to hook up with? The last idea, I rule out immediately. The others, though, launch all sorts of confusion. Even before Mom, I wasn't exactly what anyone would call experienced with the opposite sex. And since then I've been in emotional hibernation. Other than GC, who's more of a girlfriend than anything, my friend count has gone to zero. And though I haven't really thought of myself as lonely, that's how I feel when I think of Burt and of me walking away from him.

Then a thump on the floor shocks me awake. The light's all wrong, and the ceiling's too far away until I remember where I am. My journal's fallen off the bed. That's what woke me. When my heart is close to normal I turn off the light and settle onto my pillow, eyes open to the darkness, concentrating on my breath.

Something taps. I lift my head. "Come in?" But the

sound hadn't come from the direction of the door.

A breeze flutters the pages of my journal. Something's creaking, like a heavy object swinging.

"Who's there?" I snap the bulb back on, but the room's normal.

With my pillow for a shield I dash to the window. Tall trees spread black and gray over the yard, but no branches come anywhere near the window. The last time I remember seeing so many stars I was curled in the sand with Mom, her hair perfumed with sunscreen and salt and wood smoke.

Easing myself back under the sheets, I tense my toes and count to ten. I flex my calves, then my thighs, contracting and holding and relaxing the way Dr. Spangler taught.

The desk chair scrapes across the floor, but I can't see what's moving it. A scream catches in my throat, and I hear the voice again. *Help me.* I retreat to the head of my bed, shrinking against the wall. My heart's pounding, but I can hardly breathe. The wind gusts again, and the leaves of my maple tree flicker green in the moonlight. The desk chair teeters backwards, hovers on two legs, then slams to the floor. I hear the creak of old wood, like a boat in a storm, and *help me* caresses my ears.

Then I'm alone, scanning from corner to shadowy corner, gasping for breath as I sob. I want to yell for Grandpa, but I'm afraid of what I'll say and what he'll hear. I'm wishing Burt hadn't said the house was haunted. Then again, I'd rather believe that all this, whatever it is, really is ghosts. But then again, only crazy people believe in ghosts.

The next afternoon I'm sitting at the kitchen table, trying to work on my history paper, but there's the whine of power-tools, and my thoughts keep spinning back to that voice, the chair on the floor. I'm trying to believe that the wind blew it over. Or maybe it was an animal, or the floor's uneven, or the house settling made it fall. But none of that explains the voice. The obvious answer is that I've inherited whatever Mom had, but I'd rather believe in ghosts. Maybe it's Mom haunting me. Then again, maybe it's just the opening rounds of a condition that will toy with my brain until it drives me to my own violent end. I lay my head on the cool table and imagine telling Mom all this, and how she of all people would understand. On a good day, at least. And my head aches from the hammers and buzzsaws, and I haven't written a single word, and Grandpa comes in from the back yard.

"Forget school for a little while," he snaps his shears for emphasis. "Some fresh air and good, old-fashioned, hard work will clear your mind." In Grandpa's world, fresh air and hard work can cure anything. And I'm willing to believe it, so outside we go.

Grandpa hands me a saw and a brand new pair of gloves and points me to a thicket he claims is a holly hedge and tells me to cut them back.

The bushes are taller than I am, with fierce thorns. "How?" I ask.

"Hard."

I absorb the pain and hack away years of neglect. Mom would love this. The old Mom, that is, the farm girl who coaxed blooms from abandoned orchids, drew fruit from dried-up trees, and transformed our urban home into a lush jungle.

Soon I'm sweating through my shirt, my arms are crosshatched with gashes and dried blood. My shoulders ache, but in a good way. And I don't know how much time passes but when I get to the end of the row I realize I haven't thought about the nightmares for the longest time in what feels like forever.

I step away and stretch my stiff back. Piles of branches surround the skeletal hollies. I've gone too far, and regret surges through me like after the Witch moved in and I let Mom's plants die. It would've been easy to keep them alive; Mom left impeccable feeding and watering schedules, but if Mom wouldn't stick around to help them, then why should I? And since the Witch doesn't tend to anything but herself, the leaves yellowed and curled, one by one, and dropped. I thought it would be satisfying, watching them die, but seeing the house stripped of its vegetal heart just made me bitter.

Since then, the only thing that grows in our house is resentment. The Witch resents me for being bitchy and rude. I resent her on principle. Dad resents us both for being so stubborn, and I resent him for not taking my side. Dr. Spangler calls it a negative feedback loop and tells me to find a productive way to express my anger. Coloring my hair green was as close as I came.

Grandpa takes a break to survey my massacre.

"Do you think I killed them?"

"They'll be fine," he says. "Few weeks, we'll have a fresh, green fence."

"Whoever used to live here wasn't much for gardening."

"I expect," Grandpa turns the hose on one of his new trees, "the neighbors will appreciate a new look for this place."

"That reminds me," I say. "I met a boy in town who said he talked to you."

"You mean Burton. He wanted me to hire him for yardwork."

"You told him about me?"

Grandpa smirks like he's getting the wrong idea. "I might've mentioned you."

"What, exactly, did you tell him?"

He turns the hose on the potted herbs, and the air scintillates with mint, and it's summers in the garden at the beach. "I told him to be on the lookout for my intelligent, sophisticated granddaughter who was coming up from the city."

"Is that all?" I let the compliment pass. "I mean, did you say anything about my ... situation?"

"You mean about your school troubles and whatnot?"

"Yeah." I hear the pain in his voice, but it feels good to remember I'm not the only one. "And about Mom."

"Those strike me as topics you should put out there on your own terms."

"You didn't tell him any of it?"

"Nope."

I lean against him to say thanks, but my insides churn at the idea that Burt's ghosts comments have nothing to do with Mom, that I had unloaded on him for nothing. I wonder if he'll even listen to me long enough to apologize.

I'm about to ask Grandpa if he knows anything about this Dorothy Stirling person when Grandma calls from the porch, "Better clean yourselves up. The concert starts in an hour."

I don't know about any concert, but Grandpa explains that the town sponsors a summer series in the square, and Grandma wants us all to go. I'm filthy, I'm gross, and I'm exhausted. I'd rather jam my finger down my throat than go sit in some stupid park with Grandma. But I consider Dr. Spangler's plan, and going to a concert with my grandparents, maybe even meeting some people my own age, seems like what a "normal" person might do. So

I shower and brush my hair. It's faded, but it's still pretty green. "A healing color," was Dr. Spangler's assessment, and with three words transformed my protest into a memorial.

In the kitchen, Grandpa has the table covered with three-ring binders and rows of photos and plastic placards from his new plants. "I didn't take you for a scrapbooker." My cheery tone surprises even me.

"Seed book."

"Sounds fascinating," I say, not meaning to sound so sarcastic.

"Never underestimate the power of science." Grandpa slides a photo of the butchered hollies into a clear sleeve.

"That's not science. That's arts and crafts."

"Call it what you want. These journals are helpful."

I don't need to be convinced of the benefits of a journal.

"When it comes to breeding you need reliable records. I wouldn't have gotten so much when I sold my herd if I hadn't kept good stud books."

"Do I dare to even ask what a stud book is?"

"Herd registries. Some of the pedigrees went back fifty generations."

Grandma pokes her head in. "The Giles are coming up the walk."

"Who're the Giles?"

"Your grandfather and I were talking." Grandma angles her head to see out the front door. "About how you said you wanted to meet some of the other kids?"

I nod. "Why are you whispering?" Grandpa scrutinizes his seed book and pretends not to hear any of this.

"We agree," Grandma continues. "But ..." She smoothes her skirt, which looks fresh off the ironing board. "Your grandfather might have misunderstood, and ... "

A knock sounds from the front door. A woman calls, "yoo hoo."

Grandma leans in close and says even quieter, "the son," she glances over her shoulder. "He may seem odd, but try to be nice." Then in a loud voice, as if she wants the Giles to hear her, she says, "I understand he's at the top of his class. I'm hoping he'll be a good influence."

I used to be at the top of my class. "Maybe we can be study buddies," I give a syrupy smile and brace myself.

Mr. Giles looks pleasant enough. Mrs. Giles carries a picnic basket and pretends not to give me the once-over. Behind them, still grass-stained, comes creepy, cute Burt.

chapter three

I mumble through the introductions, and Burt and I linger behind the grownups as we walk to town. I'm flummoxed by how impossible it is to apologize. It was so easy in my head, but I can't even begin.

"You try to bathe the cat?" Burt's looking at my shredded arms.

"It's from gardening," I shrug.

"Looks painful."

I wish I'd worn long sleeves.

Burt goes on. "How are you liking good old Warwick?"

"Fine, I guess." Pure conversational genius.

"Seen anything good so far?" he asks, shoving his hands into his pockets.

I don't know if he's back on the Dorothy Stirling's ghost thing, but I'm not about to tell anyone I'm hearing voices, so I muster a noncommittal "not really" noise.

"Sorry about yesterday," Burt says.

I feel even more like a jerk for not apologizing. I focus on not tripping on the roots pushing through the sidewalk.

"I shouldn't have said that stuff about your house being

haunted." He drags his hand along the bars of the iron fence.

"Don't worry about it," I say.

"I didn't mean to strike a nerve."

"You didn't." Is a lie you tell to spare someone's feelings still a lie?

"Everyone says I lack empathy."

"It's fine." For some reason I can't apologize back.

"I'm an idiot to bring up ghosts after what you've been through."

I stop. "What?"

Burt stops, too, surprised by my tone.

"What, exactly, have I been through?"

Burt makes some uncomfortable-sounding noises and looks anywhere but at me and says, "Your mother?"

"What about my mother?"

"Your grandmother explained—"

"What did she tell you?" The adults are half a block ahead of us, but they turn around.

Burt gapes. "Nothing," he says.

"Bullshit." I square my shoulders. "What did she say?"

"She told my mom that your mom died, and that you were having trouble in school and stuff, but—"

"I can't believe this."

"Mom said she wasn't supposed to tell me."

"That's how it works, though, isn't it." I'm walking again, either to take this up with Grandma or to hide my face from Burt. "Nobody tells anybody, but everybody knows." I can't hide the hitch in my voice. "Before you know it I'm 'the-girl-whose-crazy-Mom-killed-herself.'" I let him catch up because I can't really have this conversation with Grandma. "And before long I'm fat and drooling in the loony bin." We don't talk the rest of the way.

The square is perfectly Norman Rockwell, and not too far away a mother smiles and looks away as if she wasn't staring. Burt and I hardly glance at each other while Grandma and Mrs. Giles spread a blanket. Awkward doesn't begin to describe it, and I'm glad for the distraction when Mrs. Giles asks me to pour the lemonade.

"Sanford Jubilee Pavilion." Grandpa's reading the sign on the bandstand. It's set into a trellis woven with crimson roses.

"It's acoustically perfect," Mr. Giles says.

"See that name a lot around here," says Grandpa.

"The Sanfords founded the town," Mr. Giles said. "First of them came over in—"

Burt's mother clears her throat and gives him a look I interpret to mean "please spare these nice people your boring stories." Mr. Giles stops talking, and Mrs. Giles says, "Zeb fancies himself a historian."

"Or a know-it-all," Burt says to me, and I'm relieved we're talking again.

"If you stand in the right spot under the dome," Mr. Giles goes on about the bandstand, "you can project your voice clear out to the edges of the valley."

I wonder how far a voice could really reach.

"Josiah Sanford founded the village. The family's had their hands in just about every bit of industry and institution around here."

"We saw the new hospital," Grandpa adds.

"That was Ezra Sanford's baby." Mr. Giles says. "A modern renaissance man: physician, businessman, research scientist. Spent a few terms as mayor, too."

Grandma smiles politely, and I have the feeling she's bored.

But Mr. Giles keeps on, "Made a fortune in genetics. Rebuilt the hospital just before he died."

Mrs. Giles passes a plastic container of fried chicken.

"Sanford House is the oldest building in town." Mrs. Giles points beyond the Town Hall to the gray, stone mansion where Burt was mowing.

"It's Leo's house now," Burt says.

"And how is the last Sanford?" Mr. Giles asks.

"Stranger by the day," Burt says.

"Poor thing," says Mrs. Giles, offering Grandpa a devilled egg. "It must be so hard for him."

"Being super-rich?" Burt says this through a mouthful of chicken.

The house is dark in the shadow of the mountains. The grass is still striped from Burt's mower.

"I mean being all alone in the world," Mrs. Giles finishes her thought.

"He lives there all by himself?" Grandma asks.

"Turned eighteen in May," Burt says. "Officially guardian-free."

"I heard he's not doing too well in school." Mr. Giles says.

I've overheard my own name enough to despise gossip, but still I find myself staring at the dark windows, wondering what's inside.

"His parents bit it when we were kids," Burt says. "And since his uncle's croaked ... " His voice evaporates under his parents' glares, and I seethe when I realize they're shutting him up because of me, as if I'll shrivel at the mention of dead parents. Dr. Spangler would remind me *they mean well*, and I sip my lemonade. It hurts, though.

Mrs. Giles says to me, "I'm sure what Burt meant was—"

"My mother bit it, too, remember?" I cut my eyes at Grandma to let her know I know she told them.

Grandma's lips tighten, and I regret my snotty tone. The sun's behind the mountains now, and in the twilight I can at least pretend it's not uncomfortable. The pavilion lights come up. A white-haired man steps into a spotlight, and his voice booms: "The Hilltop Harmonizers." Everyone claps as four men take the stage in straw hats and striped blazers. Barber-shop quartets are the lowest form of *a capella*.

The bass begins to hum. Burt rolls his eyes. Three other hums join in.

I look to the sky, wondering if it's possible to drown

myself in a cup of lemonade.

By the end of the first song, I'm willing the atmosphere to coalesce into clouds, for a bolt of lightning to end this. Burt bumps my elbow and says to his parents, "do you mind if Ingrid and I go to the arcade?"

Permission granted, I follow Burt through the picnickers to the shops around the square. The sidewalk's crowded with vendors peddling slushies and mylar balloons. The air's rich with cotton candy.

We enter a storefront with mirrored windows, and inside's all funhouse lights and chaos. Basketballs ricochet off strobe-lit hoops. Skeeball machines spit tickets at kids' ankles. Bells jangle against the violent clatter of air hockey.

"Whack-a-mole?" Burt suggests.

The idea of hitting something appeals, so we face off across a table with nine holes between us. I wield a mallet. Burt slots a pair of quarters, and the machine blares godawful music.

A purple mole pops, and I pummel it. "Are all the concerts that bad?"

"That's one of the better ones." Burt pounds a pair of moles.

"Kill me now." I clobber another.

"A lot of kids usually show up," Burt says. "No one

actually watches the concerts."

I thump a string of three. "Cool."

The music stops. The moles have surrendered.

"There's another reason I wanted to bring you here," Burt says, and I feel an awkward moment coming. "I wanted to apologize."

"Again?"

"For that comment back there." Burt's face is red and a garish blue. "About Leo's parents."

I couldn't count the times I've snuck out to the beach house to stand on the pier where we released Mom's ashes, but the wound still isn't scabbing over. And this guy has to keep poking it. "I know my mom's dead, so you don't have to remind me of it every five minutes."

"I know, but ... " The way he tilts his head, trying to make eye contact over the whack-a-mole table, is too much.

"But what?"

"Don't you want to see her again?"

It's all I can do not to scream.

"Wouldn't you like to talk to her for just—"

"Shut. Up." I punctuate each word with mallet blow on the table. "Dead." Whack. "People." Whack. "Don't." Whack. "Come." Whack. "Back." Whack.

"Hey," an attendant shouts. The room goes quiet. "Take it easy, Thor."

Elbow-high twerps giggle at my rage. I fling the mallet and storm out. A handful of teenagers on the sidewalk stop talking and watch me.

I collapse onto a bench and pretend I'm not breaking down. A gaslight flickers over me. Burt's hovering, but I'm not looking at him. I listen to The Harmonizers harmonizing in the acoustically perfect bandstand. My cheeks dry in the air.

"How long do you think he's been waiting to use that "Thor" line?" Burt says.

"You must think I'm a lunatic," I manage.

Something behind Burt catches my eye. It's a guy coming our way, golden hair perfectly unkempt, smooth skin over subtle cheekbones. I sit up, remind myself to breathe, and pray that my face isn't totally blotchy.

"What'd you do to her?" The guy's talking to Burt, but he's looking at me. He holds a box under his arm, leaning for balance.

"Give it a rest," Burt says.

Dr. Spangler would remind me I'm not ready for a relationship yet, but I'm trying to rationalize the idea that dating is part of being normal.

I look to Burt, hoping for an introduction.

"How can I rest?" The guy smiles at me, "with you upsetting the tourists." His eyes are ice blue, and they attract like black holes.

Across the street, One of the guys nudges another guy and nods toward Burt and me and the golden-haired guy.

"I'm not a tourist." My voice barely escapes my lips.

The guy's expression softens. "I see a white cheek and faded eye," he says, "but no trace of tears."

The words are familiar, but I can't make sense of them.

"Come join us at the pit." The golden-haired guy says to me. He winks at Burt, pats the box and swaggers over to the group across the street.

"What's his deal?" I fake annoyance.

"That's Leo," Burt says. "He has issues with self-confidence."

Two girls across the street tilt their heads together, watching Burt and me. Leo high-fives the guys, then they all head down an alley between the arcade and an antiques shop.

"Friends of yours?" I ask Burt.

"Kids from school."

"What's the pit?"

"Nothing," Burt says.

He's a terrible liar.

"You offered to show me around."

"You declined."

Then it hits me, why he doesn't want to go with them. "You told them about me."

"I didn't."

"Prove it." I stand. "Let's go." I make for the alley, and

my stomach tightens at the idea of barging in alone. But if they're talking about me, I want to be in on the conversation.

chapter four

Burt relents, and he takes me to a trail into a forest. It's fully dark now, with only slivers of moonlight on the leaves. I smell wood smoke, and voices filter through the murmur of insects and the rising rush of water. We emerge into a clearing, a bluff overlooking the river. Silhouettes shift against a fire, their features resolving in orange as we approach.

A guy in a baseball cap stokes the fire with a metal rod. Sparks plume and flutter and carry up and over the water. Another guy with white-blond curls reclines in a folding chair.

A fallen tree serves as a bench, and a girl in cutoff jeans and a white t-shirt stretches out on her back, her long hair glossy in the firelight. The tip of a cigarette smolders over her lips.

Another girl sits cross-legged on the ground, lighting matches from a box and tossing them into the fire.

Leo stands at the feet of the glossy-haired girl, ripping tape from the cardboard box. He sees us and says, "Welcome to the pit. Everybody, say hello to the new girl." The group makes a collective mumble that could be obedience or mockery. He tears open the box.

"This is Heather," Leo gestures to the match girl, "our resident waif."

Her head pivots atop her ballerina-straight spine. She flash-smiles and gives an unenthusiastic wave. On a scale of one to ten, I give it about a six for sincerity.

The curly-haired boy leans around his chair to check me out. "I'm Jeff." He waves as his eyes drift from my face to my legs. "That's Toby," he points the brim of his hat to the guy with the poker. "You can call him Nitwit."

Leo continues, "and this is Angel."

The smoking girl is sitting up now. She gives me a whatever smile. Her face is kind of careless and beautiful, but her eyes are sharp somehow, and my hand instinctively reaches for my locket.

"Her bite is worse than her bark," Leo says.

"Guys, this is Ingrid," Burt says. "She moved here with her grandparents."

I don't know whether to correct this or not. But I'm thinking that if Burt's playing like he hasn't told them about me, he's doing a good job. And if it's true, it would mean that twice now I've gotten angry at him for something he hadn't done.

"Who are your grandparents?" Angel asks.

"They're new," Burt answers. "They bought Judge Stirling's old house."

"I thought that place was condemned," says Toby, stabbing the fire with the poker as he steps from rock to rock around the fire.

"My grandparents are renovating," I say, uneasy at all the attention.

"That old man was nuts," says Jeff, digging through a cooler.

"He was not," Burt says.

Jeff produces a bottle. "I found him one morning on his porch, drunk as a monkey, bawling about how his dead wife stopped talking to him." He levers off the top.

"He felt her spirit in the house," Burt says.

Jeff pings the bottle cap off Burt's head. "My point exactly."

Leo drags a chair over for me. "Our friend Burt, you see, believes our entire town is haunted."

Leo's comment reminds me that I should've given Burt the benefit of the doubt, and I'm wondering who else around here believes in ghosts. I realize I'm staring at Jeff, because he offers me the beer.

"Thanks," Angel takes the bottle before I can react.

"We'd have more," Jeff says, glaring at Toby. "But Nitwit got my ID nabbed."

"It's okay," I say, and I sit.

"Let me guess," Angel gives me a look like she has me all figured out. "You don't drink."

I'm not about to go into the effects of alcohol on brain

chemistry or the concept of isolating variables to identify reactants. Then again, I'm not going to let some upstate snark off easy. "What if I don't?" I ask.

Jeff throws me a lifeline. "She can't be too goody-two-shoes if she's out with Bugs Burton."

"Shut up, Jeff," says Burt.

"We're not together," I say.

"Has he invited you on a stakeout?" Toby says with a smug smile.

"Did you show her your lucky charm?" Angel raises the bottle to her lips.

"Guys, cut it out," Heather says and snatches the bottle from Angel.

"Yeah, guys," Jeff says. "Cut it out. You're making Heather embarrassed." Everyone but Heather and I are amused at the way he says "embarrassed."

"You guys are jerks," Heather throws a match at Jeff, who laughs and jumps out of the way.

"Maybe some wine will settle her down," Angel says.

Heather shoots her a middle finger.

"There isn't any wine," Jeff says. "Thanks to Nitwit."

"Relax, everybody," Leo removes a hardback book from his box. "Our Canadian friends send their best." He shakes the book by its spine and tosses it onto the flames.

Leo shakes another, identical book and tosses it onto the fire. Its cover reads: *History of Warwick and Environs*, by Ezra W. Sanford, MD.

"Can I see one of those?" I ask.

"Absolutely not," Leo says. He shakes a third book before feeding it to the flames, then a fourth.

"Seriously?" I'm curious about the crazy—or haunted— judge who owned my grandparents' house.

"You don't want to read this." Another book crashes into the fire.

"I do," I laugh and wonder if making me beg is just a way to hold my attention.

"This," Leo thumbs the pages, "is my uncle." He holds up a picture of a man in a lab coat. "And this," he lofts the book, "is his reminder to us all that the wholesome perfection of our fair village is the product of the noble Sanford dynasty, most notably, him. And this is not the truth." He pitches it onto the fire, blazing high, hissing and popping.

"You sound so proud," I laugh.

"Don't get him started," said Heather.

"I'm as proud of him," Leo shakes another book, "as he was of me."

I grab for the book in his hand.

"I'm sure you can find a copy in town," he says and yanks it away. "And if you do, please do us all a favor and destroy it." He opens the book and finds a compartment cut into the pages. He removes an envelope and tosses it to Angel.

I swallow hard and pretend not to smell the weed.

"About time," Heather says.

Even without Dr. Spangler's rules, I can't risk any excuse for the Witch to send me off to rehab. From the envelope, Angel extracts a bulging plastic bag. From her pocket she pulls a handful of empty baggies. Mere proximity to the drugs has my heart racing.

Leo places the box on the fire then turns to me. "As fascinating as the history of Warwick may be," he says, pulling his chair close to me and sitting, "I'd rather hear your story."

Angel's divvying up the weed into the smaller bags, but Leo's statement gets her attention, and I catch her sharing a look with Heather.

"Who are you, Ingrid?" Leo asks. "And what brings you here?" His attention is as embarrassing as it is flattering.

"Down, boy," Heather says to Leo.

"Seriously." Angel kicks Leo in the shin in a not-joking sort of way. "We know you're desperate, but give the girl some space." She walks around the circle, handing a bag to each of Toby, Jeff, and Heather.

A bead of sweat rolls down my ribs, and I wipe my hands on my shorts.

Angel sparks a lighter and holds the flame, hissing like a blowtorch, over a pipe in Heather's mouth. Heather takes a long drag and offers it to me.

I look at Burt. "I should get back."

"Of course you should," Angel says.

"Give her a break," Heather says, smoke leaking out as

she tries to talk and hold her breath.

Burt takes the pipe and cups one hand around Angel's as she puts the lighter to the bowl.

My breath has gone shallow, unproductive. "I have to go now." I stand and turn, looking into the darkness for the trail.

"I'll show you the way," Leo says.

I'm thankful for his help, but I get the feeling he planned this all along.

"Don't get carried away, kids," Angel calls as we leave. "We'll be checking on you very soon."

I can barely see as we move from the bright fire to the dark woods. I'm trying to follow the crunch of Leo's steps, but my foot snags and I crash to the ground. I hear Leo stop, then his hand finds mine, still tender from gardening, and sets off a quiver in my stomach. He helps me to my feet, and I'm embarrassed and in heaven over the fact that he keeps holding my hand while we walk through the dark forest. Finally we come out onto a street I don't recognize.

"Where are you taking me?"

"To see Mother." He drops my hand, and I fall in beside him.

"Unless you think Burt will mind," he says. "And don't worry. Angel doesn't like him."

My heart pumps out emotions I can't name.

"Of course, that could change," he says, "now that a pretty new girl's interested in him."

I would have preferred "exotic" or "intriguing," but my shoulders relax anyway, and my breath comes a little easier.

"I'm not interested in him," I say, wishing it didn't sound like I'm making an opening for Leo, but he doesn't even acknowledge the statement. "Really," I say. "Where are we going?"

"The rose garden."

Leo heads into a wooded park. A warning tickles the back of my skull, but I follow him. We cross several streams and end up in a clearing with a gazebo overgrown with roses, their blooms glowing white in the moonlight. The stream glitters and flows into the gazebo. Leo waits for me at an arched entrance, and he lets me enter first.

The gazebo's intimate, filled with the sound of running water. Through an opening overhead, our own, private moon shines in our own, private sky. We bask in silver and shadow. A girl, sculpted in bronze, kneels beside the stream. Water spills from her cupped hands into a pool of lilies.

"Ingrid, this is Mother."

"She's awfully young," I joke.

"She was nine when she modeled for the sculpture," he explains. "My grandparents commissioned it as a memorial to the locals killed in World War II."

I almost ask where she is now, but I remember. I wonder

what it's like to have your name on buildings, to have a statue of your mother in a park. In the girl's face, I see a more fragile version of Leo. The water is icy on my fingers. "She's beautiful," is all I can say.

Burt said Leo was getting stranger by the day; Mr. Giles said he was failing in school. I want to think these traits make us similar, but I can't let myself believe gossip. I try to form an opinion based on his actions: he rescues me from a dangerous situation, he brings me to meet his mother, he asks me who I am. My heart accelerates, and I try to return the favor.

"What's it like?" I ask, unable to look at him as I pry. The bronze radiates a pleasant chill, and I imagine this girl growing up, and I wonder how she died. "What's it like being you?"

"Very demanding." I sense sarcasm. He sits on the ground beside me.

Super-rich, was Burt's word. "I bet." I return his sarcasm.

"It's harder than you think." He bumps his shoulder into mine. "Having people scrutinize you, waiting to feast on your failure."

The sarcasm's turned sad, or it's a calculated move. I don't know which. But I won't pity him. "It can't be all bad," I say. "Your life, I mean." I'm still swirling from his shoulder brushing mine.

"What kind of person would I be if I complained about my life?" he asks.

My heart wobbles, and a dozen foolish responses bubble to mind. In the stream, a fish hovers, its tail flicking just enough to move neither forward nor back, just letting the water pass.

"But what about you?" He asks again. "What brought you to our little utopia?"

I could trace the events back to the moment I opened the garage door and found her, but I won't scare him off with the details. "I'm visiting my grandparents."

"How long will you be here?"

"Just till school starts." This morning it felt like a life sentence. Now it seems too short.

He stands and wanders around by the stream. "I don't even know your last name."

I stand and extend my hand in mock formality. "Ingrid Van Hooten."

He takes my hand, but instead of a handshake he bows, touching the tip of his nose to the soft part of my wrist. "At your service, Ingrid Van Hooten." I wonder if he can feel my pulse. He circles me with measured steps. "Tell me something about you."

I follow him with my eyes. "Like what?"

"Something unique."

"I once held my breath for a hundred and nine seconds." I have no idea why this comes to mind.

"Impressive," he says, still circling. "Now tell me something shocking."

"What if nothing's shocking?"

"Make something up."

"I failed every one of my classes last term, and I have been uninvited back to school unless I make up a ton of work this summer."

"If that's shocking," he strokes his chin. "It's because you seem like one of those girls who mopes over an A-minus."

"And I'll bet you make honor roll without cracking a book."

"Not exactly," he says.

I cross my arms in a thinking pose, let my eyes dip to his muscled calves, "Soccer?"

He laughs. "Not exactly a team player."

I'm getting an evasive vibe, but at least we're talking about him, not me. "Not a jock," I say. "And not a scholar." I'm looking for a clue in his face, but I lose my train of thought. "Drama?"

"I love the theater—" he clasps his hands and faces the sky—"But alas—" He drops his head—"not destined for the stage."

I laugh. "Do you always follow your destiny?"

"An excellent question," he says. "But weren't we talking about you?" He drops his dramatic pose and sits on a bench, patting it for me to join him. I sit. He touches the ends of my hair, and I resist the urge to pull away. "Green is certainly a statement," he says, "but of what? You claim to be on the verge of being kicked out of school, yet you're elegant and charming."

Light must be radiating from my skin.

"Perhaps there's been some disruption in your life, some emotional derailment?"

I go from excited to nervous, wondering what he knows, or what he can read about me.

"A bad breakup?" he guesses.

"Why would you guess that?"

"Only someone on the rebound would go on a date with Burton Giles."

"It's not a date."

"What do they call it where you're from?"

"I think the official term is 'getting set up by your grandparents with the only kid they know.'"

"But you like him."

I might admit to 'curious about' but not to 'like,' and not to Leo. "He's nice for introducing me—" I stop myself from saying *to you*—"to your friends."

"Always willing to help a pretty girl, that Burt," Leo says. "But has he bothered to try to get to know you?"

I could point out that Burt chose getting high over me, but I've already misjudged him twice. "I haven't given him much of a chance."

"I'm glad," he blinks. "Because I'd like to be the one to figure you out."

"Good luck with that." I laugh.

"I don't need luck." He slides his hand so it barely rests

against mine. "Just time."

The sound of girls singing comes from outside the gazebo. They're doing a barcarolle whose name I can't remember, but I know it's a tough piece because a couple of seniors impaled themselves on it at a student recital two years ago. The voices grow louder, and with them comes the reek of marijuana. Angel, Heather and Burt crowd into our space. Heather's polishing the soprano, and Angel's doing a decent job at the mezzo. I'm embarrassed that I'm jealous of, or maybe intimidated by, their talent, and I wish they'd ask me to join them.

They stop singing, and Leo claps a few times.

"Told you they'd be here," Angel drops onto the bench beside Leo.

Leo offers her a mint from a tin. "I'm conversing with our new friend."

"Burt told us all about her." Heather says.

I bristle at her laughter. "How kind of him," I say.

"All I said was that you live in the city," Burt clarifies.

"He wouldn't shut up about you," Heather says.

"If I didn't know any better," Angel drapes an arm around Leo, "I'd say you might have some competition."

Burt lies down on another bench. "Shut up, Angel."

Heather makes an unballerina-ish guffaw.

"I'm glad you find this so amusing," I say to Heather.

"I'm not laughing at you," Heather says. "I'm just zonked."

"You all are interrupting," Leo says. "We're playing 'getting to know Ingrid.'"

"Trying to get the lay of the land?" Angel asks. "Penetrate her façade?"

"I'm having no success whatsoever."

"You're a pig," says Angel.

"We're just talking," I say.

"You and I should talk." Angel looks at me. "Before you get any ideas about this one."

I don't know if it's supposed to be a warning or a threat, but I'm not intimidated. "So, talk," I say.

"He'll lavish his attention on you, tell you you're the only girl in the world, that you hold the key to his heart."

Leo's expression all but admits Angel's charges.

"But don't fall for it."

"Oh, really?" I say.

"Seriously," Heather adds. "He has no heart."

"Ouch," Leo fakes like he's been stabbed.

Angel continues, "He's a spoiled, little monster." She jabs him in the ribs. "What he can't buy, he charms."

"And what he can't charm," Heather says, "he takes."

"I don't get everything I want," Leo says.

"Burt," Heather says, "tell her we're right."

Burt stares at the sky.

"Giles," Angel snaps her fingers, "you in there?"

"He does have a bit of a reputation," Burt says.

"And I thought we were friends," Leo says to Burt.

"But he doesn't get everything he wants," Burt says.

There's a boom overhead, and fireworks crackle, red, against the stars.

Burt sits up. "I've gotta go."

I want to stay, but the normal thing to do is to go with Burt, so I stand. "See you guys later?" I say this generally, but I'm talking to Leo.

Heather and Angel share a look.

chapter five

The next day, the workers are bashing away downstairs. Nothing's taking shape, history-paper-wise. Instead, I'm listening to the ticking clock and trying to justify violating Dr. Spangler's rules about waiting until I'm stabilized—whatever that means—before I get involved with boys. The thing is, I'm feeling pretty stable. I didn't hear any voices last night. And the thought of Dr. Spangler's rules makes me think of my journal, and last night's dream returns to me. I'm on a train and it's dark, and there's a woman who I can't see clearly for some reason, but I know she's Mom. She said to follow her, and I cried and couldn't say anything. I should be happy it didn't wake me up this time, but the sadness is back in full force. I try to ignore it, but it's impossible, so I try to believe it's only a dream.

In addition to Dr. Spangler's rules, we made a list of goals. One of these goals is for me to develop trust in my judgment. This means making good decisions. So I'm thinking, maybe it's time to break out of the easy decisions and start the real process of moving forward. I've already sort of started to make some friends. And Dr. Spangler can't expect me to spend my entire life single. I'm supposed to learn how to be in a relationship. I have to start somewhere.

A heap of debris slides down the chute and crashes into the dumpster, and it occurs to me that maybe my history paper topic is right in front of me. Maybe there's something interesting in this town, or this neighborhood or even this house I could research. So already, I'm proving my brain is back on track. My emotions are ready. I'm ready. And I have the sudden strange feeling of happiness.

I'm even happy to hear Grandma coming up the stairs. I'm thinking of how pleased she'll be when I ask her advice on my paper, how nice it will be to have a normal conversation with her. Then she opens the door, holding the postage-prepaid mailer, and I want to fling myself into the dumpster.

"I need something," she says, as if I don't recognize the urine kit I brought with me, one for each week, just like I promised Dr. Spangler.

Knowing Grandma's outside the door makes it hard to go. But I hand over the warm container for her to sign with the date and temperature. I imagine the thing on the front porch with the outgoing mail, and I wonder who besides the postman will see it.

The whole peeing-in-a-cup ordeal pretty much kills my

mood for hanging around with Grandma. So I head to the backyard, prepared to exchange some yardwork for some grandfatherly insight.

I turn soil like a pro, and Grandpa's glad to have a helper. "Did you meet the people who lived here," I ask, "before you bought this place?" My shovel clangs against a rock.

Grandpa tells me the previous owner was a judge named Leroy Stirling. I know this already, but I don't interrupt. According to the neighbors, Judge Stirling had let the house fall apart around him. It's been empty since he died, so no wonder it's in such bad shape.

As if on cue, another load of debris crashes into the dumpster, sending up a mushroom cloud of dust.

"Do you know anything about him?"

"He was a widower. Apparently lived his whole life here."

I stab the compacted soil. "What happened to her?" I stand on the blade. "The wife."

"Never thought to ask," he says. "Why so curious?"

"I'm desperate for something to write about for my history paper." I lever out a shovelful and take a step back and stab again.

"You should talk to Archie MacLeish." Grandpa says. "Town Historian. He found me the original plans for the house."

Another shovelful of dirt comes loose. "Do you think he'd mind?"

"Probably appreciate the company. I get the impression that the Historical Society doesn't get a lot of visitors." He looks over my shoulder. "And speaking of visitors."

Angel's just rounded the corner of the house. She's wearing the same cutoff shorts she had on at the pit. "Hi." She gives Grandpa a firm handshake. "Your grandmother said you were back here," she says to me.

After her attitude last night, I'm skeptical when Angel asks if I want to go sightseeing. A film of dirt clings to my sweaty, sunscreened skin. But of course I say yes.

Angel and I start down the road. The sky is bleached white, and I'm sticky from the digging. Dirt rings my nails.

"So why are you here?" she asks. "Your parents hate you, too?"

It's an aggressive opening, but maybe it's the "too" I'm supposed to hear. "My dad's in Singapore," I say. "On business."

"Lucky you," Angel says. "How about your mom?"

I take this to mean she doesn't know. "No clue." Technically true, in that it would be impossible to say with precision where her ashes settled.

"Finally," Angel's exultant. "Someone around here with some real damage."

I make a laugh-type sound I hope conveys some understanding of whatever Angel means.

"You a cutter?"

I almost panic for a second, wondering how she knows about my razor, but she means my arms. "Gardening accident."

She just nods. I get the impression she doesn't believe me. "I wasn't even close."

"Close to what?"

"Guessing why you came to Warwick. Heather bet your parents went on a second honeymoon, *sans enfants.*"

"That would be pretty funny," I say. "Since *ma mère a était avec enfant* for her first honeymoon." My accent is still an A-plus.

"Ooh, la la." Angel says, then she's quiet for long enough for me to wonder if she thinks I'm a showoff, but she finally says, "I'll bet that went over well with *grandmère.*" She rolls her eyes back at the house, and I imagine that conversation, Mom telling Grandma she was pregnant.

"I hope you don't think we're bitchy," Angel says in a way that means not "I hope you're not offended" so much as "I hope you can deal with it." She tugs my sleeve to turn me down a side road. "We talk about everybody."

The truth was, I hated being talked about at home, where I'm That Girl Whose Mother Killed Herself. Today, though, I'm kind of liking that people are talking about me. I feel included, like I'm just a regular girl. Then a horrible thought hits me. "What was Burt's guess?"

"Well well," she says with a look like she's stumbled over a gem. "Why do you ask?"

"Just curious." I peel my shirt away from my back and get a little chill.

"Maybe you can get him to invite you on one of his 'ghost hunting' expeditions," she make air quotes, "you can ask him yourself."

"Ghost hunting?"

"I mean, since you're so curious about him."

We reach the square and cross the park. There are paths, but Angel walks straight across the grass.

"He was obviously into you last night." The way she cuts her eyes brings a rush of blood to my face. "And," she draws out the word, "He's easily in the top five."

"Top five what?" I ask.

"Top five what-do-you-think?" She says with a look like I'm the biggest dunce. "I get that he's a little peculiar." She flicks my green split ends. "But who isn't, right?"

"He said my grandparents' house is haunted."

"See? Told you he likes you." As soon as I hear this, I realize it's not Burt I want to talk about.

"Who else is in the top five?"

"Hold that thought." We stop in front of a plain but dignified house facing the square. Angel pushes through a white picket gate, and waves for me to follow her up the sidewalk. A plaque beside the front door reads, "Gardiner House, 1875."

Angel walks in like she lives there. My damp skin pebbles in the air-conditioning. The foyer's huge and empty except for an antique desk displaying pamphlets. A wide staircase curves up to the second floor, it's banister polished by a thousand dead hands.

"Hello?" Angel calls into house.

To the left is a parlor painted robin's egg blue, with a piano and a harp but no people. The room on the right is dark wood and bookshelves, and underneath the sharp furniture polish is a hint of old leather.

"Anybody home?" Angel calls again.

A wrinkled woman shuffles in from the back, her sneakers squeaking. "Welcome to the Gardiner House." Her voice is like rustling paper. She opens her mouth to continue, but nothing comes out. She's staring at my hair.

"We hear that Heather Marley gives great tours," Angel says too loudly, as if she's summoning her.

"I'll get this, Mrs. Barnes." Heather's coming around the staircase dressed like a pilgrim or something. "Welcome to the Gardiner House," she says. "Second oldest residence in Warwick."

"We can't wait to hear all about it." Angel smirks.

"Be sure to tell them about the curse," said Ms. Barnes.

"Of course."

"And the duel," the woman's voice becomes lurid.

"Yes, Mrs. Barnes," she says, then, turning to us, "right this way." Heather guides us into the library and recites a spiel about how old Mr. Gardiner made his fortune growing onions in the rich, black soil of the valley. Angel mocks Heather in pantomime, and I'm baffled about why we're here.

"And if you'll follow me upstairs," Heather says, "We'll pay a visit to the nursery."

Heather ushers us to a room with four small beds and four matching wardrobes. The sun gleams through windows that look out over a boxwood maze.

"I so hope there's a comment card at the end of this," Angel says. "Because you are doing an amazing job."

"Sorry, I couldn't get off work," Heather takes a last look down the hall then follows us into the room. "Did you tell her yet?" she asks Angel.

"I thought it'd be better coming from both of us."

"Tell me what?"

"I'm sorry," Angel says. "But Leo Sanford is off limits."

I wait for the punch-line, but the girls don't crack. "What are you talking about?"

Angel says, "I saw how you looked at him last night."

"You can't tell me who to date."

"You're right," Angel concedes. "But hear us out. You might agree it's for the best."

"I didn't do anything wrong."

"We've all been there," Heather says.

"We set up the GALS embargo for a reason," Angel says. "The boy needs to be taught a lesson."

"The GALS embargo?"

"Girls Against Leo Sanford," Heather explains.

Angel continues. "For years now, Leo Sanford's been having his way with every girl in town," Angel explains. "And, frankly, we've had enough."

"So, nobody is supposed to date him?"

"I know what you're thinking," Angel says. "Leo's rich, good-looking, charming. Everything a girl could want. But you have to forget about him."

"He's a serial heartbreaker," Heather says.

"Maybe you thought I was kidding last night," Angel says. "I wasn't. His game is simple. He showers you with attention, gives you the fairy tale princess treatment, then poof," she snaps her fingers, "it's over."

"He's on to the next girl," Heather says.

"You can't believe a word he says," Angel says. "In fact, it's safe to assume that everything he says has been intricately calculated to get into your pants."

Anxiety ripples through me. So much for trusting my judgment.

"Don't look so glum," Angel says. "It's not like you can't talk to the boy."

"Right," Heather adds. "We're not saying he's not nice."

"He has a generous heart," Angel says.

"He just needs a lesson in ... " Heather considers her words, "self-control."

"So, before you become the next girl, consider joining our embargo."

"What if I don't?"

"It's completely voluntary," says Heather. "But don't say we didn't warn you."

"And don't expect to be very popular among the female population."

Shoes squeak in the hallway.

Heather gestures out the window to the gardens. "And there," Heather's back in docent mode, gesturing out the window to the gardens, "is where the famous duel took place." Mrs. Barnes noses into the room. "Herman Sanford and Josiah Gardiner, at odds over a section of farmland, resorted to sabers at midnight on New Year's Eve, eighteen-twelve."

Angel works her hands like puppets behind Mrs. Barnes's back, but Heather's in the zone.

"Mr. Gardiner stabbed Mr. Sanford in the chest, thus setting in motion the legendary Gardiner curse."

"Tell us more," Angel says, her hand to her cheek.

Heather doesn't miss a beat. "The curse first visited the Gardiner family with the untimely death of Josiah's son during construction of the rail line. Next, Josiah's grandson fell from a cliff and died while hunting in the mountains. And finally," Heather pauses for effect, "the curse finished the family with the murder of Josiah's last heirs: his granddaughter, Dorothy Gardiner Stirling and her unborn child, poisoned by her maid, Francesca Moss."

The name Stirling is like a hammer to my forehead, and I hear the girl begging for help in my room. In the present, standing in the Gardiner house, I see Mrs. Barnes clapping, but the sounds come between beats. My hands tingle, I grasp for support, but I'm falling, and then I'm gone.

chapter six

Angel and I are sitting in the square. I'm trying to ignore my headache. Angel's plucking dandelions and pulling the flowers apart with disinterested calm. "I don't mean to sound alarmist," she says, "but that was pretty messed up."

I don't know if she means me collapsing or me coming to and sprinting out of the place before Mrs. Barnes could call my grandparents. "That'll teach me to skip breakfast," I say.

"Are you sure you're okay?"

I'm sure I'm not okay, but I tell Angel I am. Fainting is a new symptom, and I'm trying to recall links between fainting and mental illness. Also, I'm angry that nobody bothered to mention that Mrs. Stirling was murdered in my house.

"Judge Stirling believed his dead wife was talking to him, right?" I wonder where this leads. Just before I recovered from my faint, I had this dream: I'm in my room in my grandparents' house, and there's this man—it's someone I know in the dream, but not in real life—and he's just come home from work, calling out for someone. He calls over and over, and he comes up the stairs as I'm going down the stairs and I'm crying. There's a woman on the floor. The man sees her, and he looks at me. The woman's hair covers her face, and her hands cover her womb. I indulge myself for a moment. "Burt thinks Mrs. Stirling really is haunting my house."

"Just tune him out when he gets going on his ghost thing," she says. She has to lean over to pluck another dandelion. "We all do. Focus on those perfect arms."

"Do you think Burt's right?" Was her skin cold when he touched her? Why am I seeing this so clearly?

"I knew you two would be perfect together," Angel says. "It'll make it easier to stick with us GALS." She hugs me in a way that I think's supposed to be friendly, but also feels like I'm being bossed around.

I couldn't see her face in my dream, but I know she was pretty, even in death.

"Do you know where the Historical Society is?" I ask.

The Warwick Historical Society occupies a one-story brick house with arched windows and a coat of arms over the door. Inside I find a sunny central room. A faded oriental rug makes the silence seem even quieter somehow. Glass cabinets line the walls, and while the air is fusty with old books, the cabinets contain taxidermied raccoons and pigeons and brass instruments that might be old navigational tools or torture devices.

A door on the far wall stands open, and inside I see the corner of a desk. I make a tentative "hello," and chair springs complain in reply from the office.

A tall man appears, gray. His shirt is wrinkled, but his face, just dignified lines around his eyes. "Welcome." Half-glasses hang at his chest. "Can I help you?" He has an easy manner, relaxed even in his vest and tie, and he's too polite to notice my hair.

"Hi. I'm looking for Mr. MacLeish."

"And Mr. MacLeish you have found." He could voice Santa Clause in an animated special. "And what may I do for you this fine summer morning?"

"I'm trying to find some information about a house in town. My grandfather said you might be able to help."

I begin to explain where I live when he interrupts me.

"Your grandfather must be Karl Bruni," Mr. MacLeish says. "We're thrilled that he's restoring the place."

I wonder who "we" are, and what else "we" know about me, but I say, "I'm more interested in the former owners."

Mr. MacLeish nods like he knows where I'm going. "The Stirlings?" he asks with hesitation.

I nod back, and we're both nodding.

"Come in," he indicates his office. "Have a seat." The way he avoids eye contact reminds me of my headmistress just before she broke the news about me maybe not returning to school next year.

He settles in his chair and squares a stack of papers. His desk is buried in journals, books, mail. I'm wedged into a hard wooden chair between his desk and more bookcases.

The window's bright behind him, illuminating the dust on three framed diplomas. A photograph shows a younger Mr. MacLeish in a tweed suit and round wire glasses, and in the picture he's being hugged by the no-lie President of the United States.

"I was surprised that your grandfather didn't bring it up," he says.

A ceramic stein with the Harvard crest hold two new pencils and two pens.

It takes me a few seconds to realize he's talking about the murder. "I heard some rumors." I feel ghoulish. "I was wondering if you know where I might find the truth."

"*Veritas vos liberabit*, as they say."

"Do you think you might be able to point me in the right direction?"

"You're already here."

I force a polite laugh.

Mr. MacLeish gives the broad strokes of Dorothy Stirling's life: how she moved into the house when she married Judge Stirling. Her father was judge when they got married, and her husband—Judge Stirling—succeeded her father on the bench. Mrs. Stirling was pregnant with their first child when their maid poisoned her. He pats his desk with both hands like "that's that," and I get the feeling he doesn't want to talk about it.

"What was she like, Mrs. Stirling?"

"I moved here later, but they say she was a beauty. Popular girl. Tragic. They'd hadn't been married a year. Judge Stirling—" his voice quiets, and he begs my pardon before he removes a handkerchief and spends a moment polishing his glasses. "He was a good friend. Came home from work—he wasn't the judge then, yet, and ... " He doesn't have to finish.

I've already seen it. For the second time today I feel like I'm falling. I blink back into my chair, and Mr. MacLeish's staring at me, his head cocked like a bird.

"May I offer you a glass of water?" Mr. MacLeish says.

"Do you think she's still there?"

"Excuse me?"

"I heard that Judge Stirling said ... " I frame my words carefully to be sure the idea is someone else's not mine. I don't want to say this at all. "Did he think she was haunting him?"

Mr. MacLeish smiles for less than a second. He rubs his hands, rotates his chair slowly to one side then the other. "I know ... " He leans forward onto his desk. He looks at the ceiling, and I want to run away. He thinks I'm a stupid kid, and he's trying very hard not to laugh in my face. He exhales, and he's composed again. "People often say things after ... " His eyes meet mine, and I can tell he's being careful, too.

"After an unpleasant experience."

"Do you think—"

"Wait," His hands are up, palms toward me, trying to soften the interruption. "Whatever his reasons, Leroy Stirling was a good man. And I won't judge him."

"Do you believe him?"

He holds my gaze for a moment. His mouth turns downward and his face sags. I wonder if he's feeling sad for Judge Stirling or pitying me. "I believe the past offers much to instruct us, and I believe the first step toward true knowledge is to study those who came before us. But, no. I don't believe in ghosts."

His certainty should have relieved me, but I feel like he's leaving something out.

"This is for a history paper, you say?"

"A murdered bride and a haunted judge," I say. "In my grandparents' house. It seemed like it might be an interesting topic."

"But are you sure you want to ... " I don't try to finish his sentence. "Do you think it's fair to him?"

"Do you think he was—" Manners prevent me from saying *mentally ill* "—imagining it?"

"I won't pretend to know another man's mind," he says. "But we all have our own perceptual prisms. In truth, he was letting things slip. The house, for example, he wouldn't do a thing to it. The place was nearly falling down by the time he died."

"But you don't believe in ghosts," I keep my voice low. "So you don't believe Judge Stirling."

"I—" He stops. "How—" He drums his fingertips together and blinks. "There are some in our town who like to play up the 'haunted' elements of Warwick. It's exciting. It attracts tourists." Another pause. "But at the Warwick Historical Society, we deal in facts."

His tone is stern, and while I don't entirely believe Mr. MacLeish, for some reason I like him.

"These people," I say. "The ones who say there are ghosts. Who, exactly, are they?"

"When presenting your work as *historical* ... " His sudden seriousness draws me forward. "When writing about actual men, a historian is advised to confine her treatment to proven, verifiable facts."

"Of course," I say, and I mean it. "But if he said it himself, Judge Stirling, that is, isn't a historian obligated to at least investigate the idea?" Dr. Spangler would be so proud of me right now. "So surely you know someone?"

Mr. MacLeish frowns and takes a pencil. As he writes he says, "He's as bright as they come, but he's undisciplined, intellectually. Don't let him corrupt you." He starts to hand me the paper, but when I laugh, he pulls it back. "Be discerning," he's looking dead into my eyes, "as you seek to sift history from hogwash."

Burt isn't home, but Mrs. Giles tells me he's mowing the grass at the cemetery. I'm sort of not surprised that he works there, but I am surprised when Mrs. Giles says to tell my grandparents she looks forward to seeing *Hamlet* with them tonight.

Normally I find cemeteries vain and annoying, but this place is peaceful, with gravel paths that wind among the hedges and gravestones. The shady trees and benches might make it a good escape from my grandparents. I scan for Burt and listen for a mower as I wind further and further among the dead.

The cemetery seems to be arranged concentrically, and I grow kind of dreamy reading the headstones, entire lives reduced to names and dates and a few words. One grave's marked only with a mound of dirt and matted grass. Some stones are barely legible. The deeper I walk, the higher the hills and the more elaborate the graves. I wonder which are the one-and-a-half percent who killed themselves. I wonder how many of the suicides were found by their daughters.

Dad wanted Mom buried, but, thanks to Grandpa, Mom got what she wanted: to be cremated and scattered in the sea, to be free. Even so, Dad insisted on a monument, so he ordered a headstone and set it in the graveyard of some church. He says it's important to have a place to go to remember her. I've been there exactly once.

Through a break in the trees, I spot the pyramid. From the road it looked big; up close it's impossibly enormous.

Sheer planes of polished stone reflect the trees and the sky. I trail my fingers along the seamless granite, my eyes following the vertices, rising razor-straight.

I turn a corner to see Burt yank the starting cord of a mower. The engine sputters but doesn't start. A red, metal tool box rests on the grass beside him.

"Your mom told me you'd be here," I say.

He turns to me but doesn't smile. "Leo bored with you already?"

"Mr. MacLeish suggested I talk to you."

He kneels to fuss with the motor. "What about?"

"About Mrs. Stirling?"

He becomes still, but doesn't turn to me.

"Why didn't you tell me about her?" I ask.

"When?" He fishes a wrench from the toolbox, "While you were yelling and pounding on the table, or when you were running off with Leo."

"Sorry." I say.

Maybe my apology surprises him, because there's an awkward pause, and when he finally says, "no biggie," I feel even worse, like I'm just another in a string of disappointments.

"Did you ever—" I'm struggling for a way to ask this without suggesting I believe in ghosts, but without offending him, "—meet her?"

"She died in, like, the sixties." He fits a wrench over the head of a bolt.

"But Mr. Stirling saw her." I add quickly, "you said."

"He thought she was still there." He strains to turn the wrench.

"Did you ever see her?"

"No." The bolt comes free, and Burt's hand bashes the motor. He rubs his knuckles and curses under his breath.

"But you believe she's real?"

"I believe the Judge."

Burt's loyalty makes me like him. I press on, "Have you ever seen a ghost?"

He studies the part he's removed from the motor. Blood beads on his knuckle. "Sadly, no."

"But you believe they exist."

"The universe is full of things we can't explain." He chucks the part into the toolbox. "Shouldn't we try to figure them out?"

"Is that supposed to be Romantic?"

"I'm a scientist," he says.

I make a scoffing noise through my nose.

"You don't think you can use scientific methods to study supernatural phenomena."

I note his proper use of the plural. "Do you believe Mrs. Stirling is haunting my house?"

"The judge described a classic, level-one manifestation."

"Meaning?"

"Indirect contact. Cold spots. Lights turning on and off."

A week ago I would have bit my lip at his earnestness.

"Objects moving on their own." Burt blots his knuckles on his jeans. "He heard her once."

And I hear her, and despite the heat, a shiver grips me. My head swims, and I take hold of the mower handle for support. Burt asks what's wrong.

I balance trust against fear. "Can you keep a secret?"

"Depends."

"No." I harden my expression. "You absolutely can't tell anyone."

"Sure."

If this gets back to Dr. Spangler that's one thing, but if the Witch hears that I'm hearing ghosts, I'm done. "If you tell anyone, bad things will happen to me."

"Like what?"

I want to punch his incredulous grin. "Not one single person."

"I promise."

"I think Mrs. Stirling is haunting my house."

He shakes his head and turns back to the motor.

"Did Leo put you up to this?"

"He has nothing to do with this."

"Angel then?"

I'm confused. "Mr. MacLeish said you were an expert."

"MacLeish doesn't believe in ghosts."

"I need your help," I say.

"Let me guess. You want me to come over, set up my

equipment, and hide in the dark until the spooky noises return."

I have no clue what equipment he's talking about. "If that's how it works."

He throws the wrench into the tool box. "And then everyone shows up and finds me hiding in the closet with a suitcase full of cameras. You have no idea how I got there. Everyone laughs, and I'm in violation." He slams the metal lid.

"As much as I'd like to delve," I say, "I need you to believe me."

He hefts the tools and heaves the mower forward. "Whatever."

"I'm trusting you," I say to his back. "This could seriously ruin my life." He keeps walking. "Now you have to trust me." I jog to catch up. "The other night my desk chair flung itself across the room. Then—" I hate to do it, but I force a sob. "I keep hearing this woman begging me for help." The tears appear on their own. I wipe my eyes and my voice comes out a whisper. "I have to find out the truth."

Burt shows up at the kitchen door at precisely nine o'clock, carrying a hard, silver case in one hand and a *Buffy the Vampire Slayer* lunchbox in the other. He wears a black canvas backpack with a tripod strapped to the side.

"Bring enough stuff?" I ask.

"I brought all the gear I have."

I take the silver case and start up the stairs.

My grandparents are with the Giles on their way to Chatham. It took some serious begging for them to let me stay home alone, but I told Grandma I spent the afternoon at the Historical Society and didn't want to lose momentum on my paper. I guess I sounded genuine enough, because Grandpa backed me up, so she relented and left me at home to work. *Hamlet's* scheduled to end at midnight, so with the trip home, we'll have a fair amount of what Burt calls "peak hours."

My room's organized in anticipation of his visit, but having a cute boy just a few centimeters from a drawer full of my bras and panties kicks me off balance in an excited way. The fact that doing all this in secret, not to mention that we're trying to videotape a ghost, sets off all sorts of alarms. We aren't doing anything wrong, but then again neither were GC and I.

Burt does a quick survey: the desk with my school books arranged by height, the dresser, my hairbrush, my bed. He lifts my maple off the windowsill, gives me a questioning glance and sets it on the dresser. "Can I just say," he unfolds his tripod. "how excited I am to finally be here?"

I can't tell if he means my bedroom or my haunted bedroom. He assembles his gadgets with practiced hands. The night air pulses in through the window, cooler but humid. Alone with Burt and his clean soapy smell that doesn't conceal his earthy boy-scent, I realize I'm happy that he's here, too.

"I'll show those numbskulls from GHAST once and for all." He looks to me for affirmation, but I'm baffled. "I can't believe I used to want to join them."

"Who?"

"GHAST. I applied four times."

"I give up. What's GHAST?"

"The Ghosts, Hauntings and Spirits Team."

I shake my head.

Burt goes on. "It was me who convinced Judge Stirling to hire them." He twists a lens onto a camera, checks the viewfinder. "And they had the nerve to tell me to shove off, that I wasn't 'professional.'"

He mounts a video camera on the tripod, explains how it's rigged to capture 360-degree images. "I'm just as professional as those losers."

I resist asking why he wants to join a bunch of losers. Even though he comes across as a total dweeb, his enthusiasm tells me I'm in good hands.

I half-listen as he explains the electromagnetic field detectors. One, he says, detects a wide range. The other's tuned to typical household frequencies. Somehow—he's pleased with himself—this will tell him whether an EMF anomaly is just an air conditioner coming on, or something outside the norm. "Isolating the variables," he says.

"My therapist does the same thing with me," I say. I'm not sure why I want him to know this.

"You on any drugs?" He says this like he's not surprised, like maybe everyone's in therapy.

"I don't even drink."

"I mean like antidepressants or anything."

"No," I say.

He sets a thermometer by the window, another on the desk along with an old cassette recorder and tells me that analog tape catches sounds that don't always show up on digital recordings.

He snaps the latch on the Buffy lunchbox. "Behold," he says and extracts a device from a foam cutout. "The Spectrans 920M."

It's so dorky it's cute. "What's it do?"

"Full spectrum, HD A/V capture and transmission."

"Like I said. What's it do?"

"It's like an high-definition camcorder on steroids. It sees a ton more than the human eye, from infrared up to ultraviolet, a hundred-eighty degree field of vision out to fifteen feet. Dual mic's and twenty-four-bit-wave EVP capture." It looks like a joystick with a lens and a camera at the top. "Sensitive enough to see the heat off a gnat, and powerful enough to transmit all the data wirelessly back to the mothership. If your ghost shows up, this'll see her."

"I can see I chose the right man for the job," I say.

"We'll show those idiots at GHAST who the real ghost-hunter is."

I'm considering whether he actually believes we'll show this to anyone, whether he gets that me seeing dead people is not something I can have out in the open.

"Where did you hear her?" he asks.

"I don't know. It's like she was just in my head." I'm glad Dr. Spangler doesn't hear me say this.

"I mean where were you."

I point to my bed and cringe a little as he stretches out where I sleep, panning the spec-trans and looking at the screen. I wonder how long the smell of his hair will linger on my pillow.

It's fully dark by the time the setup's complete. He hands me a flashlight and a handheld recorder.

"What's this for?"

"Digital voice recorder," he explains. "Voice-activated. Transmits to my computer. For backup, really, in case we get separated." His hand touches mine as he switches on the device. "Say something."

I speak into the device, looking at him. "How, exactly, would we get separated?"

"Maybe you get carried off by an evil spirit."

"Funny," I say. "But speaking of that, what do we do if someone shows up?"

"If it seems friendly, we try to communicate."

"I mean my grandparents."

"I'll explain that I'm here for strictly professional

purposes." Burt adjusts a dial on the Spec-trans.

"Not sure that'll save you."

"They'll think we're up to no good?"

"Having boys in my bedroom is kind of a hot-button issue."

Burt's catching on, and I'm sensing jealousy in his silence.

"Not exactly my first offense."

He doesn't look at me, but asks if it was worth it in a voice that makes me feel bad for letting him think the worst.

"He was just a friend. He needed a place to crash."

"That's what they all say."

"The look on my stepmother's face when she saw him shirtless in my bed was priceless."

"Your shirtless friend," he says, "in your bed."

I like that he's jealous, but I don't want him to think I'm a slut. "He's gay."

"I'm sure your stepmother believed that."

"She was just happy to have an excuse to get rid of me."

"If your grandparents come home early," he leans out the window. "I can make it to the scaffolding."

"And your stuff?"

"Just toss my shirt under the bed."

I punch his surprisingly solid shoulder. "I mean your cameras, perv." I feel like a schoolgirl when I realize I hit him just to touch him.

"You're the one with naked gay guys in your bed."

"I knew I shouldn't have told you that story."

"You absolutely should've told me that story," Burt says. "I was beginning to think you were a total prude."

"Well, if my grandmother finds video cameras all over my bedroom, 'prude' is not the word she'll use."

"Shove them under the bed, too." Burt switches off the light. "With my shirt."

We settle onto the floor, because sitting on the bed with him in the dark would be too much. We both jump when something hard hits the windowpane.

Burt puts his finger to his lips.

Another tap, then, a thump on the floor. I scream in spite of myself. A rock skitters against the wall.

"Sorry," comes a voice from the backyard.

Burt scrambles to the window. "Who's there?" he calls.

"Giles?" Leo Sanford's voice from outside.

Burt drops to the floor. "You set me up."

"I did not."

"What's he doing here?"

"I should ask you the same thing."

"Am I interrupting something?" Leo calls.

I look out the window. "What are you doing?"

"Is Burt with you?"

"Hang on, I'm coming down," I call. I whisper to Burt as I move to the door, "Did you invite him?"

Burt shakes his head. "Do you want me to come with you?"

"No." I gallop down the stairs and outside to the back porch. Leo appears from behind a ragged shrub. "What are you doing here?" I say. "You scared me to death."

"I missed you."

I want him to say this over and over, but I can't right now. "You have to go," I say. "It's not a good time."

"Was that Giles up there?" Leo smirks and points at my window.

"That's none of your business."

"Don't tell me you fell for his haunted house ploy."

"It's not what you think," I lie. "I can explain."

"I'm all ears." He edges closer.

"Later," I say. "You need to go."

"First," the space between us shrinks further, "tell me one thing."

"What."

His nose is inches from mine. I want to taste his candy cane breath. "When you kiss him, do you picture me?"

"Leave now." I push him, but in a playful way. "Or I'll never speak to you again."

"Wow," Leo backs away. "They were wrong about you."

"What's that supposed to mean?"

"Later," he waves and turns.

I want to follow him into the dark, but I just breathe deeply, wondering why he chose tonight to come to my window. I'm thinking about what Leo said, and by the time I'm upstairs I'm boiling. "I trusted you, Burt."

Burt's lifting his multi-lensed video camera from the tripod. "I trusted you." He places it into its case.

"You're telling me you didn't tell Leo about this?"

"Why would I do that?"

"Why would Leo say I fell for your haunted house scam?"

Burt flushes. "Why don't you ask him?"

"I swore you to secrecy."

"I kept your secret."

If Burt thinks I invited Leo for some reason, it means he didn't tell him. This idea sinks in, that a charming guy chose to visit me in the middle of the night. He'd risked getting caught by my grandparents, maybe the police, just to see me.

Burt says, "You swear no one put you up to this?"

I point the video camera at myself and press 'record.' "I, Ingrid Van Hooten, do solemnly swear that I invited Burt Giles," I pan over him, "to my room, alone, with no adult supervision whatsoever in the middle of the night." I switch off the camera. "There," I say. "If I'm lying, email that to my wicked stepmother."

"Thank you," he says, and I feel like we're back on good terms.

"If I see that on the internet, you and I are going to have a serious problem."

"Don't worry," he says. "Now let's find your ghost."

And we're sitting in the dark, and I can feel him breathing next to me, and it's strange that I'm in a dark bedroom with a cute boy and, like with GC, it's perfectly innocent. Noble, in a way, for him to join me on this search for something that can't possibly exist. Anyone else would think I was crazy. But the "ghost hunting scam" comment keeps coming back to me, and I wonder if this is all a ploy, Burt's plan to get me alone. And if it is, then why isn't he trying anything? "I'm not a prude, you know."

"You don't have to whisper," Burt says.

"I've actually done some seriously un-prudish things."

"Sure you have."

"When my mom died, I went a little wild." I don't know what's making me say this. I just want him to think I'm normal. "I skipped a lot of school, tried just about everything I could get my hands on."

The clock ticks seven times before he responds.

"Doesn't seem like you."

"That girl's gone." I squeeze the locket through my shirt. "I think."

"That's why you don't drink?"

"Therapist's orders. No alcohol, drugs, boys, cigarettes."

"I love how you throw boys in there. Like boys are a bad habit."

"I'm supposed to be focusing on me."

"What would your therapist say if you told him you

were sitting in the dark with a guy, trying to film a ghost?"

"First of all, she's a she. Second of all, I would never in a million years tell her I thought I heard a ghost."

"I thought you were supposed to tell your therapist everything," Burt says.

"It's complicated," I say. I try to imagine what Burt'll do if I tell him Mom was mentally ill, that she committed suicide. Then, before I second guess myself, I tell him. I let the words flow out before I can even hear them, much less stop them. And in the silence that follows, I think about how many people actually know this even though I've never said it out loud. "That puts me officially 'at risk' for the same thing."

"You seem pretty sane to me."

I could float away. "My doctor says so, too," I say. "But what do you think'd happen if I told her I was hearing voices."

"For what it's worth, I believe you."

I scoot closer. My room isn't frightening at all with him here. In fact, I want the woman to turn up just so Burt can see it, so she can be real. I'm thinking it would be nice if he held my hand or put his arm around me, and I'm wondering if falling for two boys—if that's what I'm doing—means I'm not ready for one, when she whispers, "*Wake up.*"

I bolt upright. "Did you hear that?"

"*I'm running out of time.*"

I shiver at the cold sound, as real and formless as the

insects buzzing outside. I try to speak but a wheezy groan emerges.

"What's going on?" Burt says.

"Who are you?" I have to concentrate on each syllable.

Burt's looking around. "Who are you talking to?"

She hovers overhead, swaying against the dark ceiling. Long dark hair, black eyes, her face is girlish and shines from within.

Every cell wants to flee, but I can't. The room fades, and I see only this person, this woman, this girl, suspended before me, her eyes burning with terror and sadness, igniting terror and sadness inside me. I can no longer feel the floor.

The woman reaches for me, her movement distorted and slow. Her black lips move, and it feels like forever before *please help me* tickles my ears. She shimmers in the darkness, translucent white eyelids and a gauzy gown, floating in a slow rotation.

My lungs are useless. I gasp and to my horror reach to meet her hand, but the shade is gone, the woman is gone. Part of me has gone with her.

"Ingrid, what is it?" Burt demands. "What are you pointing at?"

My heart's chugging. I'm panting but breathless. "Did you see her?"

"What's going on?" Burt's voice is panicky.

"Her."

He's at his laptop, scrolling back through the feed from his sensors. "I don't see anything."

"She was there. She's running out of time."

"I think I fell asleep," he says, his fingers flying over the keyboard. "Oh crickets! It's almost two a.m. I've gotta get out of here."

"No," I grip his arm.

Burt scoops up cameras, thermometers, EMF sensors.

"Don't leave me."

But he slings his backpack and makes for the stairs.

I force my heavy legs to follow, gripping door frames and walls for balance, swatting on light switches as we pass.

"Please stay," I grab his shoulder.

"I have to get home before my parents," he's bubbling over. "But I'll go through the captures tonight."

I'm coming apart and he's giddy.

"If she was really here, we'll be famous."

And then I'm alone, hating myself for sharing my secrets with Burt. I'm trembling, but I'm not cold. I want to call Dr. Spangler right now, but to say what I don't know. Also I'm afraid of what she might tell me. I feel as far from normal as I've been since Mom. I have no one.

chapter seven

Angel and Heather turn up the following afternoon, carrying big totes and smelling of coconuts. "Put on your suit," Angel says. Heather's bikini tie dangles out her neckline.

I've been trying to start my history paper, but I'm bone tired. The hanging woman is seared into my memory, and behind every sound I hear her cry for help. Being with the girls might clear my head, so I go with them.

We take the trail to the pit in single file. Ferns tickle my shins. The high canopy mottles the light. A cardinal flashes through a sunbeam and disappears. We reach the river, and in the daylight it's wider than I thought. We're on a bluff overlooking a wide bend. The water's deep where it meets the bluff, but on the far side, at the inside of the bend, it riffles shallow over a bed of smooth stones. The smell of ashes hangs in the air.

Heather wriggles out of her shorts. Her legs are lean and smooth, her pixie hair the color of almonds. Angel spreads a blanket in a pool of sunlight. Heather runs and leaps off the bluff and splashes into the river. Angel follows her in a graceful dive. I toe the grass at the soft, undercut edge, watching them floating in the dark water.

"Come on," Angel yells.

"It's kind of scary," I say, meaning the jump, not the water.

"Hell yes!" Angel shouts.

"Jump!" Heather chimes in.

Before I can second guess myself, I push off. The girls hoot as I drop to a breathtaking, icy shock. I sputter, gasping but proud, happy to be in the water, the familiar freedom of buoyancy.

Angel and Heather clamber up the bluff. It's harder than it looks, and I'm out of breath by the time I've hauled myself up. They're stretched out on their towels, taut and glistening. I wring my hair and lay down beside them. The sun's heaven after the cold water, and the grass is soft beneath my towel.

Angel says, "Heard you had a little rendezvous with Burt."

I try to pretend I'm not pissed that they know this. "He was helping me with a project," I say, bracing for questions about my sanity and the possibility of ghosts.

"In the middle of the night?" Angel says. "With the lights off?"

"Yes." I say unconvincingly.

Angel raises herself to her elbows. "You're telling me you had that boy alone in your bedroom and nothing happened?"

I'm relieved that they don't know about the voices, about the woman, but in a way I want to talk about it. I feel like maybe talking about it will help me help her.

Heather shifts onto her side and gives me a skeptical look.

"It's true."

"You don't have to lie," Angel says. "I'm not your mother."

This girl seems to know where all my buttons are.

"Come on," Angel gives me a friendly poke. "Just because he's a weirdo doesn't mean he isn't hot."

"He's not a weirdo," Heather says.

"Don't worry," Angel says. "I'm sure it's not genetic."

"You and Burt are related?" I'm glad to change the subject.

"Cousins," Heather says.

"So, what was all that the other night about the graveyard and the red wine?" It's a relief there's nothing to be jealous of there. I'm also confused that I'm relieved, because I don't think I like Burt that way.

"Yeah, Heather," Angel says, "what's that all about?" It's clear that Angel knows.

"Not again." Heather rolls onto her back, legs crossed.

"Come on, she's one of us now."

"It's humiliating." Heather joggles her foot.

"It's hilarious," Angel promises me. Then to Heather:

"Tell the story, or I will."

"Fine," Heather sits up and coils into lotus. "Promise not to laugh, though."

"That's ridiculous," Angel says. "She's going to laugh."

"This is mortifying." She stretches her arms, left hand pulling right wrist, then switching.

"You know we love you," Angel says.

"Okay," Heather arches her back and stretches out again onto her stomach. Our three faces are close enough I can smell the remnants of coffee. "It's last summer," she flexes her knees, her feet bouncing over her flowered bikini bottom. "And for some reason, Burt decides he needs a rabbit's foot."

"Not weird at all," Angel says.

"And of course he can't just buy one. It has to come from a graveyard rabbit, and he has to catch it during a full moon."

"Is anyone else starving?" Angel asks.

"Then cut off its foot," Heather says as she digs into her bag. She looks up at us to say, "While it's still warm."

"That's disgusting," I say.

"Think about that the next time you're working on a project," Angel says.

"And he insists I come along," Heather says.

"The mighty ghost hunter was scared," Angel watches Heather, still rifling through her stuff. "Tell me you brought snacks."

"There's no way I'm helping him dissect a rabbit. But he says all I have to do is keep him company, and he'll bring wine." Heather produces an apple. "And he builds this trap out of chicken wire."

"Just your average Friday night," Angel snatches at the apple, but Heather's too quick.

"Why I said yes, I have no idea."

"It was the wine."

"Shut up," Heather chucks the apple halfway hard at Angel. "So at some point, I have to pee, so, I find a dark spot."

Angel crunches off a big bite and says, "We're all class here in Warwick," and wipes juice from her chin.

"I have your vitamins, too, by the way, and some protein bars," she says to Angel. "And you're welcome." Then she's back to the story. "And I end up passing out with my jeans around my ankles." Even telling a story about passing out peeing, Heather's adorable. "Not my finest moment."

"Meanwhile, back at the rabbit trap ... " Angel prods.

"Have you ever heard a rabbit scream?" Heather asks. I shake my head. "It's bloodcurdling. Or so says Burt. And it's so loud the caretaker hears it and catches Burt mid-surgery."

My expression is somewhere between amused and horrified.

"Somehow Burt, who's already on probation, convinces the caretaker to let him go."

This reminds me of a question I forgot to ask Burt.

"Why's he—"

"And my oh-so-thoughtful cousin scrams, leaving me behind,"

"Exactly the right word," Angel says.

It's cozy, sharing secrets with the girls.

"He claims he thought I had already made my getaway. But no. I'm snoozing against a tombstone till the next morning when the caretaker almost runs me over with his tractor."

"Yikes," I say.

"Yeah," Heather rolls onto her back. "I'm tangled in my jeans, bare ass in the wind, and the creepy caretaker can't look anywhere near me, and all he can say is ... " Heather's voice goes deep and gravelly, "'em-bare-assed.'"

Heather's blushing.

Angel's laughing. "Don't be ashamed," she says. "You have a cute butt."

I can't remember the last time I laughed with girlfriends. It's springtime in my soul. And even though I don't think I care, I have to ask. "What's the probation for?"

"Trespassing," Heather says. "Got caught in the abandoned hospital trying to film ghosts," Heather puts air quotes around "film ghosts".

"With Margaret Baker," Angel adds. "And if you believe the rumors, she also might have had some wine, and might also not have been fully clothed."

Heather peels bark from a twig with her perfectly

shaped but unpainted thumbnail. "I heard Leo called the cops."

"Why would he do that?" I ask.

"Those boys—" Angel says. She cocks her head like a dog that's heard its master's car round the corner.

Heather shrugs, "Since when does Leo need a reason to mess with Burt."

"—everything's a competition."

A commotion from the woods gets all our attention.

Branches snap and leaves fly as Toby, Jeff and Leo burst into the clearing, bare-chested, arms pumping, kicking up dirt as they sprint. We squeal and duck as three sets of legs hurdle us in stride. The boys jostle for position until they launch themselves headlong off the bluff.

"Sad, isn't it," said Heather. "What we have to choose from around here."

The guys climb back up, all smiles. Their chests heave as they shed water. I've spent plenty of time around half-naked boys, but these guys are buff even compared to the guys on the swim team. And despite his claims of being unathletic, Leo moves like he's made of water.

Angel clutches my forearm, and I realize I'm staring. And he's staring back. I draw my knees to my chest.

"Do you mind? Angel says to Leo. "You're blocking my sun."

"Come swimming," Leo says.

I wonder if I'm violating the GALS embargo as I move

to stand up.

"We'll all go," Angel takes my hand and Heather's and we three girls leap off the bluff together. I'm ready for the cold this time, and the water's delicious. I feel my old self reviving somewhere deep. Leo cannonballs after us. Toby does a perfect one-and-a-half. Jeff tries a flip but lands smack on his back.

Leo splashes me as he treads water. "How was last night?" He asks.

"I don't know," I say. This isn't the conversation I want to have. "Different?"

Toby and Jeff are trying to out-handstand each other in the shallows.

"Different good or different bad?" Heather says.

"Just different."

"So evasive," Heather says. "Very suspicious."

"I agree," Leo says, drifting toward me.

"I told you. He was helping me with a school project."

Angel swims between Leo and me, her back to him. "I'm not buying it."

"Doesn't matter," Heather says, "Burt can't keep a secret to save his life."

I wonder what's on Burt's computer, whether he's posting it somewhere right now.

"Half of what comes from Burt's mouth," Leo says, "is pure fantasy."

"The same goes for you," Angel says.

"If half of what Leo says is false," Heather posits, "and he claims half of what Burt says is lies, does that make Burt seventy-five percent trustworthy or seventy-five percent untrustworthy?" She floats onto her back. "And if it's the former, is it, like, every fourth sentence is false, or does he tell the truth to three out of four people?" Her feet flutter. "Does he lie one-point-seven-five days per week?"

"Now who's showing off," Angel says.

Heather's on a roll. "For instance, with you, Leo, we've figured it out. You lie to half the people in the world."

"Ta da!" This is Toby, standing on one hand, toes pointed.

"Perhaps," Leo says. "But do you know which half?"

"The half with breasts," says Angel and submerges.

"She has a point," Toby says, still upside down, shoulders rippling as he walks forward on his hands to catch up with his feet before he falls.

"Don't listen to them," Leo says. "They're trying to poison you against me."

"Why would we poison our new friend?" Heather says, and hearing her say it makes me happy.

"I don't pretend to understand the mystery that is Woman." Leo jumps to one side and probes the water. "I can't even follow your math."

"I'll explain it to you later, bro," Jeff's poised quietly, stalking a fish. His back's red from the failed flip. Angel still hasn't surfaced.

"Thanks, Jeff. I take extreme comfort knowing that you have my ba—" this last word is lost as Leo's pulled under. He thrashes back up.

Angel arises behind him, dangling his red swimming trunks. "Lose something?" She flings them at Jeff, who jumps clear before they splat onto a rock.

I laugh as I paddle away. Angel sprints for the shallows, Heather's climbing the bank. I'm alone in the pool with naked Leo.

"You know, skinny-dipping is illegal," Toby says.

"Dear, kind Ingrid," Leo says, bobbing shoulder deep. "Could you find it in your heart to lend a hand?"

"Don't do it," Angel shouts.

"What's in it for me?" I enjoy the power.

"Name your price." A dragonfly hovers beside his face.

I'm sizzling with embarrassment and excitement and the surprising joy of becoming part of a group so comfortable and familiar they can terrorize each other like this, confident enough to tell humiliating stories about themselves, continually probing one other, attacking and retaliating within some unspoken set of boundaries. I almost wish the boys aren't involved, so I can just relish the girls. But there's Leo, and hanging from my fingers is his suit. "Promise to always tell me the truth."

"I'll always tell you the truth."

"He's lying," Angel says.

"All girls." I say.

"Done." Three dragonflies now flicker impossibly over the water around him.

"Don't believe him," says Angel.

"You want the truth?" Leo asks.

"The whole truth."

"Behold," Leo springs from the water. "The whole truth." He charges me. I scream and drop his suit and halfway avert my eyes as I splash away, but the image is indelible.

Jeff whoops and laughter erupts. Leo takes a bow. Heather and Angel cat-call and whistle as Leo steps into his trunks. The dragonflies have vanished.

"Dude, you're shameless," Toby's an octave higher than normal, "and awesome!"

"Leo Sanford, you magnificent stud," Jeff shouts, "I am in love with you."

"Dude, take off your pants," Toby yells in my direction.

I laugh, hoping he's joking. But Toby is looking at Burt, standing on the bluff, hands in his pockets. Burt's looking at me. His face is dark and tired. "We need to talk."

"Oooooh," Angel drones. "Looks like someone wants some more of Ingrid's project."

"*Nothing* sure is getting serious," Heather says.

Whatever Burt has to say, I don't want him saying it here. So I take the jeers and hoots, I towel off and say goodbye.

"Strike three, Giles," Leo shouts.

chapter eight

Dirt clings to my wet ankles as Burt and I walk. We emerge into the bright street and he still hasn't said what he came to say. My head's a collage of a naked boy and a hanged girl.

Burt vaults the spiked iron fence into the cemetery, and in my impatience with his overdramatic silence, I demand to know where we're going.

"I want to try something," he says.

He treads over graves with scientific detachment, as oblivious to the corpses underneath as they are, presumably, to him.

I stick to the path. The tip of the pyramid shows through the trees, beguiling in its stillness as the foreground slips past. My thoughts disengage as I walk, and I drift into an unreal world where the sun has set and the pyramid shines with the greenish-pewter of moonlit leaves. Leo is near, lured by the same compulsion that draws me, and I can't explain where I feel this force, only that it comes from the pyramid, the convergence of planes.

"We're here." It's still daytime, and Burt, not Leo, is

talking to me. About what, I can't say. We're in a family plot bounded by banks of azaleas, their leaves drooping in the heat. The ground is littered with the brown crepe of dead blooms.

"Feel anything?" Burt says. Instead of grass clippings, today he smells like fresh laundry.

"Annoyed?"

Burt takes my hands, and I give him a WTF look.

"It's an experiment," he says, and he places my hands on a headstone. "Now?"

The stone is cool. I take in the inscription—Dorothy Gardiner Stirling—and my hands recoil. "What is wrong with you?"

"Proximity to the grave is supposed to heighten psychic phenomena."

One minute, I'm goofing around, making new friends. Now, I'm violating a woman who was murdered in my house.

"I thought being here might inspire something metaphysical."

"You said you were a scientist."

"I'm trying to see if you can really see ghosts."

"I want to stop seeing ghosts!" My stark raving shout echoes off the mountains, and as my words come back at me, as I hear them aloud, my head fogs. I'm seized by the very real possibility that these strange things may simply be symptoms: voices, hallucinations, fainting. I'm teetering on the edge of a full-bore panic attack. I need to breathe, but my lungs won't accept the oxygen. My face tingles, and my bones evaporate. A bird is singing, repeating a harmonic series I could match in pitch, but I can't name the notes. I can't be this out of control, but I can't stop it.

I lean on the headstone to keep from falling. A papery rustling draws my vision downward, and a rabbit steps out of the azaleas and sniffs my foot. She takes a kind of half-walking, half-hopping step, whiskers twitching at me beneath iris-less eyes.

Burt's voice bounces around but doesn't settle into words.

The world steadies.

Burt's face is scrunched, and I realize he's been saying my name this whole time. He can't see the rabbit, and I make a note of her paws—four—and a giggle seeps out unbidden. The rabbit spooks, brushes my feet, and vanishes.

"What's so funny?" Burt asks.

Of course he's baffled by my emotional pivot. So am I, but I don't have the heart to tell him I heard Heather's story. "Nothing," I say, partly because it's probably embarrassing and partly because I don't want to confront the fact that he chopped a foot off a live rabbit.

"You are one of the strangest people I know." He shakes his head and raises his hands in a gesture of peace or maybe surrender.

"You brought me here hoping I would see a ghost when

the whole reason I shared my secret with you was so you could help me stop seeing ghosts."

"You should thank me, then."

"Why's that?"

"There's no ghost." His mouth is a line. "The video. There's nothing there. No thermal or magnetic disturbances, nothing on the tape."

"That's impossible," I say. Thinking it's exactly the wrong word.

"I checked three times." He tucks his hands into his pockets.

"But you saw her," I say.

"All I saw was you."

My arm hairs stand. "You had to see her." I sound desperate. "She was real."

"Not according to my sensors."

"I'm losing my mind." I'm as angry as I am scared.

"The Judge said he felt someone in the house," says Burt. "He wasn't crazy, and neither are you."

"You're just saying that."

"I want to believe you."

"You want to believe in ghosts."

"Let me try again." Burt says. "No gear, just you and me."

You and me I hear in my head. *You and me.*

Back at my grandparents' house, I start on my journal, but my head's full of thoughts I don't dare commit to ink. Why did I see her. Is she Mom? Is she some future version of myself? Why didn't she show up on Burt's cameras? How am I supposed to concentrate on a history paper? Why can't I get rid of that damn, mousy stench?

I sweep again. I wipe down the walls and scrub the floor, following each board back and forth, swimming laps in a deep pool. I'm swimming between worlds, one filled with the warm buzz of new friends, flickering romance, normalcy. I reverse and swim back to the woman's voice, unnerving if she's real, terrifying if she's not. Bobbing alongside: Leo, Burt and Mom. Stroke, stroke, stroke, breath. Right, left, right, breath. Thirty-six strokes, duck, flip. But I can't swim forever.

At the beach, one of my favorite things with Mom was to paddle the kayaks out past the sandbar or around the point where she'd show me places like the cliffs or the fossil beds, things that were in plain sight, but that you could never see if you stayed on land.

On the last day of summer before seventh grade, early, when the sky was pink, before the wind came up, she took me to the cove. At low tide, a broken mast pierced the surface to mark the grave of an old cargo ship. Under the clear water the barnacled hull lay on the bottom, half-buried for a hundred years.

It was loaded with pitch, bound for England, when the cargo ignited and burned until the ship foundered.

"Do you hear them?" she asked me. Her eyes were closed, her face shaded from the sun rising behind her.

I heard the gulls and the water lapping against our hulls. I was afraid Mom was having one of her episodes when the surface rippled, and a stingray shimmered beneath my boat. I gasped and stiffened as dozens more appeared.

"Mom?" I said, feeling like every tiny movement would capsize me. Every correction I made set the boat rocking worse. "I don't like this."

"Shhhhh." With an easy stroke she pulled alongside and steadied me. "There's nothing to be afraid of." Her eyes were a million miles away as the rays flowed silently beneath us, and when they passed, she put her finger to her lips. "Listen," she whispered.

We drove back to the city that night, and as I tried to sleep, my next day's outfit draped over a chair, I wondered who it was Mom heard out there in the water. I wanted to ask her, but I didn't want her to tell me. When Dad said Mom heard voices, I could believe he was wrong, but if she told me herself, I don't know what I'd believe.

The room's as clean as it's going to get. But it's been four days and I haven't so much as figured out a topic for my paper. I need to research, to write, to get this done. I give my maple a drink. At the tip of one leafless branch, a pink node swells.

I consider that the most obvious explanation is correct. My brain, like Mom's, is parting ways with reality. She met the first of her "invisible friends" when she was sixteen. She told fabulous tales about people that only she ever saw. She dropped out of college when she got pregnant and married Dad. The doctors' diagnoses changed with the seasons, but that hadn't stopped them from prescribing a flood of medicines that swept Mom from hallucinatory to catatonic, frantic to lethargic, easygoing to hypercritical, but never well. I don't want her future. I need to take control.

I need a manageable task, something simple to give me traction. So, with straight-edge and pencil I grid out twenty-one boxes, three rows with seven columns each. I label and number the days until my paper's due. I allocate hours to research, writing, editing. And somehow dissecting the project and spreading it across the calendar makes it seem doable. I find myself relaxed, proud even. I lean out my window and draw long, slow breaths of night air, confident in the knowledge that I might actually be in control. I won't see her again, I tell myself. She's gone.

I squint as I awaken. Something isn't right. The room's too bright, the colors too vivid. Shapes are bold and stark as if outlined in heavy ink. On the windowsill, the maple flashes madly against the purple sky. The node has burst, and the wisp of a new leaf pair unfurls.

I refuse to worry about the strangeness, but as I autopilot through my morning routine I figure it out: no voices, no woman, no nightmares. Not once did I wake with faceless Mom clenching my wrist, telling me to stop being afraid and to leap in after her, not a single sweat-soaked moment of Mom lunging for me, begging for me from behind the veil of her hair to join her. Sometimes I think it would be easier to go with her, to wake up with her, to not wake up at all. I hate the nightmares. But if I stop seeing her in my dreams, will I ever see her?

I head to the kitchen. Grandpa's reading the paper. I say hi and pull the corn flakes from the cabinet.

"I didn't expect to see you so early," he says.

The way he's looking at me makes me check my reflection. "Early birds and worms," I say. I look the same, I think.

"After your little escapade, I thought you'd sleep in."

I make a non-committal um, searching for meaning, wondering if he found out Burt was over the other night.

"Your grandmother was right. You were asleep."

I smile like it's nothing, but my heart's revving hard.

"You woke us up, tearing the basement apart. Scared us

half to death."

I checked out the basement my second day here, looking for another place to sleep. Once was enough.

"I thought we were being robbed," he gives a little laugh.

I convulse with a nervous laugh of my own. My face is hot.

"You asked me whose locket that was."

I swallow hard and my hand goes to the chain.

"Then you started on about how you needed rope," he laughs. "You were furious that you couldn't find any rope."

I touch my throat. I'm expecting to feel the tender remnants of a burn. I remember an urgent need, an ache like a broken bone. Time is flowing too quickly. I'm swept away by injustice, betrayal, the hunger of unrequited love, the infinite finality of being forgotten. I don't know where these sensations come from. The universe is erasing me, like the sea closing over a drowning soul.

I tell Grandpa I'm up early to meet Heather for coffee before she goes to work, and I'm calm as I leave the house. The lie tugs at me, but I have to move. My hands quiver and my head wheels between the shrinking belief that everything I've seen has been real and the looming dread that I'm reliving Mom's life.

I find myself at the doorstep of Sanford House. My

shoes are soaked from the dew. I shouldn't be here. Dr. Spangler would tell me to go home, but, frankly, I'm sick of her plan. I've completed my journal and made my bed every day for months. I've kept the routine, and I've kept the world at arm's length during my quest for normal, but I'm getting farther away. I consider finding Angel, but I have no idea where she lives. Her embargo crosses my mind, but it's time to confront my situation head on. I'm not going to let Mom get in my way.

The *gong* of the doorbell hums through the walls like a low-frequency alarm. I savor the danger, the deviation from the prescribed path. I've read the medical journals and every case I can get my hands on in search of a name for Mom's condition, for what may or may not be my condition. I've reviewed Mom's symptoms with Dr. Spangler, compared them to my own. But of all Mom's symptoms, sleepwalking wasn't one. This is something different. I've kept every appointment and subjected myself to MRI, PET scans, cognitive testing, blood testing. I haven't missed an appointment and I haven't blown a drug test. But their plan isn't working. The nightmares have escaped, they've materialized into real voices, real visions. They're manipulating my senses, my thoughts, my body. I have to try something new. If I want to be normal, I have to be like everybody else. I have to engage.

Leo opens the door. I step inside. He moves to speak, but I stop him with a kiss. The floor drops away, and I rise like the tide when I inhale his minty breath. Blood floods my fingertips, my toes, my tongue, swollen and hot with the guilt of empowerment.

He's all blinks and pink cheeks.

I touch his lips. "Shhh," I say, then stretch onto my toes to cup my hands around his ear and whisper. "This isn't happening."

If Leo is as bad as the girls say, then I must remain in control. He can't seduce me if it's my idea. Ready or not, I need to feel something real again.

"Do you have anything to drink?" I ask, holding his hands.

"Coffee?"

"Something stronger."

The ceiling creaks, and Leo says, "Let me show you the gardens."

The foyer's like a lobby, and opposite the front door is a windowless metal door with a brass nameplate that reads "Ezra W. Sanford, MD."

Leo leads me up the stairs to a hall hung with dour portraits, a pantheon of Sanford patriarchs, framed in gilt. The air feels atrophied, as if it has been sealed inside for too long. An inscrutable and dark oriental swallows the sound of our steps.

The portraits judge me as I follow Leo. The last one's not a dark-suited man, but a woman in elegant red. I see Leo's eyes, his cheekbones, and I recognize her. "Your mother."

"A few months before the accident." He takes my hand and takes me down a back staircase and outside.

The garden is exquisite, so much so that I'm awash in the joy of sharing this with Mom and the simultaneous crushing, grinding, scraping reality of the impossibility of sharing this with Mom. This garden is way too orderly for her. Mom's gardens, if they were planned at all, the design was visible only to her. I consider for the millionth time whether heaven is real, and if it's this beautiful, and if you get in if you kill yourself.

"Do you have any wine?" I ask.

"Red or white?"

Before Dr. Spangler, the question was never "what color" but "how much." I choose red to match the roses and the gate at the end of the path.

"Make yourself at home." Leo gestures to a chaise lounge, wide enough for two, beside a gnarled bonsai pine.

The lounges are inviting, but the mossy paths and low hedges draw me out into the garden, where I'm surprised to find high walls, where manicured vines and trees blend with a painted landscape to make it look like the garden isn't enclosed but open, extending for miles.

I admire an espaliered apple tree, its branches tipped with shriveled calyxes clinging to the ovaries, plumping into fruit. "This is how I felt," Mom told me as we wired the branches of a pear tree to the sunny wall of the beach house, "when I was pregnant with you." It was the summer

I turned twelve. "You literally filled me with joy," she said. I remember my ugly braces, sharp against my lips, and wondering if I would ever understand what it meant to have a baby inside me. "I felt beautiful," Mom said, "and captured." The crack in her voice startled me. She swiped away a tear and left in its place a stripe of dirt, and the aroma of mulch and the soft warmth of her arms around me bring a tear to my eye to remember.

I try to soak up the scene, to make it a permanent part of me, so I can hold this feeling forever: the white foxgloves, the pink tongues of their bells echoing the scarlet blooms of the roses cascading from the trellis behind them.

Leo returns with a bottle and glasses. He unscrews the cork while I admire the bonsaied pine. The trunk is thick and layered in crackling bark. Sharp, dead branches intersperse the live limbs, twisting into an irregular pyramid as high as my chin.

Leo fills the glasses,

"This is spectacular," I say.

"My great-grandfather started it." Leo says. "We've been training it for generations."

"Mom loved gardens." I'm surprised to say it aloud.

"They're a lot of work," Leo says. He hands me a glass.

"To your great-grandfather's bonsai." The rims of our glasses ping.

"To your mother," he says.

I drain my glass. My mouth tingles. "It's bad luck not to

drink after a toast." My head swirls, and I sit on the warm cushion of the lounge.

"Who needs luck?" he says, but he takes a sip.

"I forgot." I swallow to control my churning stomach. "Your life is all laid out for you." The spasm passes, and I ring my empty glass with my fingernail.

He refills me, and I take another gulp, then scoot aside to make room.

Leo reclines into the cushion, and I snuggle against him. Clouds linger over the mountains. A line of windmills turn on a ridge, tiny and slow in the distance. I sizzle with excitement and danger.

I lay my head against his shoulder and close my eyes, relaxing in his scent of faded sunscreen. In the phosphene glow of the sun through my eyelids, I see the pale, hanging woman, a noose pinching her neck, her black lips pleading. I open my eyes to dispel the vision. Panic shivers through me, and I wonder what exactly I'm doing here with Leo, drinking wine, while she hangs.

Leo's hand on my waist brings me back with a thrilling jolt. His fingers slide under the hem of my shirt, setting my skin ablaze. The wine buzzes through my blood, pure for so long, poisoned in a blink. I shift out from under his hand.

He sits up, looking like he's been roused from a pleasant dream. "Too much?" He asks.

My glass falls to the ground. A breeze stirs the wine's bouquet, and my thoughts thicken and slow.

"Is everything all right?"

"No." I want to tell him why I shouldn't be drinking, why I shouldn't be here at all. But I don't want to drive him away.

"What's the matter?"

Angst coils against my ribs, the discomfort of something left undone. My thoughts escape half-formed. "Everything's changing," I say.

"For the better?" he gives a hopeful laugh.

"Kiss me," I say before I can stop myself. "Before it's too late." I press him onto his back and linger in his ice-blue eyes, his graceful lashes, the warmth of his chest as it lifts and and sinks beneath me. I touch my lips to his, soft and electric. A tear forms and, before I can stop it, drops.

"Am I that bad a kisser?" My tear moistens his cheek.

I force a laugh. "It's fine," I whisper as I roll off of him. I press the heels of my hands against my eyes, holding my breath to suppress my sobs.

A metallic clack rattles the air. The red gate creaks on its hinges, and through the gate, carrying a rake and a pair of clippers, walks Burt.

"Of course," Leo says. "The lawn boy."

Burt's eyes flash from me to Leo to the wine bottle and back to me. I turn my face to the immaculate sky. "What the hell's going on?" Burt's yelling.

Leo's on his feet. "None of your business."

Burt pushes past Leo to pick up my red-stained glass.

"What did you do?"

"Get out of here." Leo grabs Burt by the shoulder.

Burt knocks Leo's hand away and kneels beside me. "She can't do this."

"You had your chance." Leo hoists Burt to his feet.

"Stop." I should be flattered, but I feel like a prop.

"How much has she had?" Burt asks.

Leo says, "What's it to you?"

"She has a condition," Burt checks the bottle and upends it. "She's—"

"I'm not—" Whatever he's going to say, I don't want Leo to hear.

"What did you do to her?" Burt demands.

I manage to stand.

"I told you to get out," Leo says.

"I'll go," I say. I'm wobbly, but I make it to the gate.

"Wait," Leo says, "I'll give you a ride home."

"I'll find my own way."

I make it few yards down the alley before I have to stop and lean myself against the wall. Leo and Burt are shouting, but I can't make out their words. My gut clenches, and my throat burns. Blessed cold radiates from the stones.

The yelling stops, and the gate slams. Burt stalks past me.

"Let me explain?" I ask.

"Explain how 'I'm not supposed to date' only applies to me."

"Please don't be mad."

"First the whole bullshit ghost stakeout, which Leo conveniently interrupts. Then you're naked with him in the river. Of course you're hooking up with him."

"I wasn't naked."

"With me you're all 'I'm too fragile to drink or date'. With him you're a—"

My stomach heaves into my mouth, and I choke it back down. Burt's walking away. When I can talk again, I say, "There's something I have to tell you."

"Tell Leo." He doesn't even turn around.

"You're the only one who believes me." I slip along the cobblestones after him.

"Not anymore."

"You were right." I say. "We have to try again."

"Why?" He keeps walking. "So you can set me up again?"

"She's trying to kill me."

"You're pathological," he throws up his arms but keeps walking.

"She—"

"Save it."

We reach the square. "They found me last night in the basement." I must look crazy.

"So what?"

"I don't remember how I got there." I hate my tears, how phony they must look. "I think she's taking over my body."

113

"A ghost made you go to Leo's house." He's mocking. "Made you to get drunk and—"

"No. That was my idea. My stupid, ridiculous idea. I had to get away from her."

"Get away from me."

"I need your help."

His eyes narrow with rage. "Then why did you go to him?"

"As soon as I was with him I knew it was wrong. I'm scared, and I could use an ally."

"'Use' being the operative word."

"Will you please get over your stupid jealousy?"

"I worked pretty hard to be your ally."

"Do you know how happy I was when you showed up back there?" I realize my nails are digging into my palms, and I relax my hands. "Please help me." I hear my words in the air, but the woman's voice in my head.

"Don't take this the wrong way," Burt says. "But you're delusional."

"You said you believed me."

"I was in your room. There was no one there."

"She needs my help, but I don't know what to do. Now she's trying to kill me. She makes me so sad, and I'm afraid I'm running out of time."

"You saw her again." It's a statement, like he's trying to pin down my facts.

"She's there, hanging by her neck, staring with her dead,

black eyes. I need to know if it's real or if I'm just ... I need you to help me."

"Wait, what?"

"Tonight. When my grandparents are out."

"Hanging by her neck?"

"Yes, in a noose, like an execution."

"Or a suicide."

My blood crystallizes. This is what she wants me to do. My stomach won't stay down.

"I don't think you're seeing Mrs. Stirling." His eyes spark as he says this.

"Can't you please believe me?"

"It's the murderer."

And then my stomach erupts and pink bile splatters the cobblestones and our shoes.

Burt tells me to wait, and he leaves, and I'm crumpled on the sidewalk for all to see: me and a gallon of vomit. I feel like a tramp, and I'm emanating a sour nastiness that turns the heads of the passersby. This is not who I want to be.

All I can do is sit there on the ground. I haven't had a drink for two hundred and twenty days. I want to tell to Dr. Spangler. I want to hear her say this isn't a relapse, not even a slip. I'm not even in treatment for drinking, yet here I am, stained with my wine-soaked puke. I'm in treatment because I'm plagued with nightmares and because I'm "at risk" for the whatever mental illness drove my mother to kill herself. But I'm not insane; I'm angry and tired and sad because my mother killed herself in front of me and I hate her from the pit of my stomach and I hate myself for hating her.

But I can't call Dr. Spangler because I won't lie to her. And if I tell her this was triggered by some murderer's ghost who's gotten into my head and is trying to make me kill myself, well, I don't want to hear the end of that conversation.

Burt returns with a bottle of water and douses my puke. He helps me to my feet. I won't look up until we're out of the square, but I'm saying "I'm sorry" and "thanks" and "I'm sorry" and "thanks." I need to check in with my grandparents, so when I'm pulled together enough he takes me home. Men are ripping off pieces of roof, and it sounds like a ship smashing against rocks.

My grandparents are waiting, but they're not freaked out like the first time I left. They seem relieved that Burt's with me. Again he lies for me, spinning a straight-faced story about how we all met for an early breakfast and some undercooked eggs. Workers clomp by with stacks of shingles. Burt asks me in front of my grandparents if I still want to go to the WHS to research my paper this afternoon.

I need to rest, so I tell him maybe in a few hours. Grandma's look tells me she doesn't like the idea, but Grandpa nods, so she doesn't say anything.

chapter nine

"This is it," Burt says, and we climb off a bus onto a causeway at the edge of town. Below the road on both sides, furrowed fields stretch across rich, black lowland. It's late afternoon, and there's no hiding from the roasting sun.

Burt starts toward a low, brick house sitting alone at the edge of the fields. The front window glows lurid pink from a neon hand, fingers spread, between the glass and the drawn curtains. The half-moon of windows in the top of the door are mirrored, and I can't even look at my spongy pores and my hair hanging limp from the heat.

With the Witch waiting to pounce on any behavior that smacks of crazy, me consulting a psychic is a terrible idea. But Burt says a scientist explores all avenues. And he reminds me there are plenty of things science can't explain, like the human brain, he notes. Or like Mom.

Burt rings the bell. A bolt clunks, the door opens, and a slice of a woman's face appears in the crack. "Oh, Lord," she drawls. She slips the chain and looks down at us with soft, moss-colored eyes. "Tell me this ain't what it looks like." Her words are velvet.

"Madame Zalenko?" Burt says, "We need help."

She's looking at me. "You need help?" I want to wrap myself in her voice.

"Yeah," I say.

"She—we need you ... " Madame Zalenko waits while Burt stammers, "to contact a ghost."

"Come on in." The door opens, and she motions for us to follow her. Burt doesn't take his eyes off her silk robe caressing her hips as she walks.

"I usually do my divining in the mornings," she says without a single "g". "But I'll make an exception for you," she means me, "out of professional courtesy."

She leads us to a pair of sofas facing each other. The air is polar and the color of twilight. The décor is high-end, unlived-in. There's a sideboard with every type of booze. More than one perfume lingers.

She reclines into the sofa opposite us and crosses her legs. Her glossy hair settles over the curves of her shoulders. "Who are you trying to reach, exactly?" When she says "exactly" her eyes flick from her fingernails to me. "Your mother?" Her mouth turns down, but it somehow conveys happiness. The violent white of an old scar bisects her left eyebrow.

I'm wanting Burt to explain, but he can't even look at her.

"You've got your work cut out with that one," Madame Zalenko says to me. Her eyes tell me she means Burt. He doesn't get it, and it's like she and I are alone, sharing a private joke. I make a little nod, feeling slightly less uncomfortable.

A moment passes. "Y'all want something to drink?" Every syllable is its own world.

I shake my head. This amuses her for a moment, then her face stiffens. She oscillates between middle-aged and just out of college. "You do realize today's Friday, right?"

Burt's mute, and I don't know what to say.

"I've got some people coming over later, so ... " I could bathe in the sound from her lips. She leans toward me in a move that connotes expectation at the same time it displays some dangerous cleavage.

"I'm being haunted." I blurt.

"I know, honey," she reaches across and lays her hand on my knee. "But what do you need me for?"

"It's a murderer," Burt says.

"Do tell," she says, in a tone that is at once dismissive of him but encouraging to me. So I explain about the voice and the vision and the sleepwalking. It feels good coming out, and even though I go on for a long time, she doesn't interrupt. In fact, she watches me so carefully I wonder if she's reading my lips, and she nods when I pause after describing the failed stakeout.

"Don't worry about what's in there," she says, and I realize I've been fussing with my locket this whole time. "I'm gonna give you a minute," she stands. Whether it's makeup or the light, her skin is sublime. "Think about what you just told me," she says, "and what you left out."

Madame Zalenko leaves down a gray hallway, and a minute or so later, choral music sings quietly from speakers I can't see. She returns carrying a silver tray set for tea.

She pours hot water over the infusers, and the air comes alive with jasmine. "Before I forget," she says, "There's a fee."

"How much? Burt asks.

"Depends on what you want." She reclines and crosses her legs. Her right hand hovers behind her head.

Burt says, "We want a ritual to summon her."

Her gaze edges toward Burt for a moment then back to me. Her thumbnail traces patient circles on the pad of her middle finger. "Summon from where?" She surprises me with a wink.

"The other side." Burt says. He still can't make eye contact with her.

"You get that out of a book?" Burt flushes, and she removes her smile. "Fifty'll get us started."

Burt sees my shock but says it's fine. He extracts a handful of bills, and with the money comes a shriveled finger of fur with long, curved claws.

She smiles at the grotesque thing. "I may have misjudged you." She says to Burt and slides the bills into her bra. "Now tell me again," she lifts her teacup with finger and thumb, "what it is you need?"

"We want to see her," Burt says, "to prove ghosts exist."

Madame Zalenko closes her eyes and inhales steam. I imagine her as a movie star or a spy or a mom, and each seems somehow plausible. "I was asking her," she whispers, eyes still closed.

"I want her to leave me alone," I say.

"She bothering you?"

I almost say "she wants to kill me," but it would sound crazy.

"I don't know what she wants."

"You girls have something in common?"

It takes me a second to absorb what she said, that I'm like the ghost of a suicide. "No."

"Most times," she says, "a spirit visits someone with a connection. Blood most likely. Sometimes a spirit's attached to an object or a place." The woman sets her cup on the table. "Is she someone you know?" she asks. "Someone from your past?"

"No." I'm with Mom in the garage, the rumbling engine, the stench and the realization. I would give anything to have one more minute together.

"Judge Stirling thought his wife was haunting him," Burt says. "But we think it's Francesca Moss."

"She kin to you?" Zalenko asks me.

"She was the Stirlings' maid," Burt says. "She poisoned Mrs. Stirling."

I'm afraid to blink because if I close my eyes I'll see the woman hanging by her neck.

"She killed herself," Burt says. "In Ingrid's room."

Madame Zalenko hums an affirmation, and her expression suggests this might have come up sooner. "Anything else?"

"She keeps begging for help," I manage to say.

"You're just gonna have to ask her what she wants."

"I'm afraid."

"Sure you are. It's tough being needed."

"What am I supposed to do?" My voice cracks.

"Help her." Madame Zalenko's voice is soothing but insistent.

"How?"

"Let her in," she says like it's the easiest thing in the world.

"How do we make her appear?" Burt says.

Madame Zalenko laughs, deep and throaty. "Doesn't sound like that's the problem." She rises to her feet. "Real trick might be getting her to leave." The hem of Madame Zalenko's gown flutters as she glides to the door. "You'll come back, right?" She dismisses us with manners so subtle but firm that, before I see what's happening, I'm standing on the stoop wondering when I left the sofa. "Next time's on the house," she says, and the door heaves to.

chapter ten

Grandma and Grandpa leave to play bridge, and Burt taps at the kitchen door. He said he wasn't bringing his gear, but he's wearing a backpack. My heart stutters when he produces a gardenia. "You shouldn't have," I say, and I mean it. But its perfume is luscious.

"It's supposed to help focus your energy."

What energy he's referring to is beyond me. Burt unwraps a crystal bowl and floats the blossom in water he says he brought from the river.

"For a scientist, you sure know a lot about hocus-pocus."

"In for a penny."

We sit cross-legged on the floor beside my bed, facing each other over a flickering candle. Wax pools beneath the flame. Burt's cheekbones glow. His shadow's huge and misshapen behind him. He holds out his hands, and I tried to act casual as our palms touch. The clock ticks off the seconds.

Following his lead, I close my eyes.

I have to bite my lip when he drones, "Fraaan–cesss-caaa" in long, low tones.

"Really?"

"Madame Zalenko said we're supposed to summon her."

The word she used was "invite," but I close my eyes and repeat her name.

We sink into a rhythm, breathing, exhaling "Francesca" in unison. Memories of chapels and Ouija boards drift past. The air is narcotic from the gardenia. I focus my thoughts on the woman. A shiver shakes my hips, I must twitch or something because Burt shushes me.

His hands are warm. The smell of his shampoo weaves through the flower and the candle and the dusty, mousy smell that I can't scrub away. I miss his grassy scent.

"Francesca." We chant in long exhalations. Burt's voice comes out an A, and I sing the E above it, out of habit, and my thoughts somehow find Mr. Owen, my seventh-grade choir instructor, and how Lucy and Nicole and I went mushy over his dimples and his Irish accent. We swore jealous allegiance against his fairy wife, who we were certain had only ensnared him through sorcery. The memories gather like snow, and I'm remembering how badly I wanted the solo that Lucy won, and how she wore her white dress so when she took the stage next to Mr. Owen we could imagine they were being married, and my head snaps upright and I realize I've just awakened.

"Concentrate," Burt says.

"Sorry." I fall back in with Burt's chanting, this time

counting the iterations of "Francesca" to hold my focus. I reach nine, and a gust extinguishes the candle.

Burt's looking at me when I open my eyes. "Did you feel that?" he whispers.

The curtains billow inward.

"Hauntings often manifest by cold spots," Burt says.

It was the wind, I think.

He re-lights the candle and closes his eyes again and I follow suit, knee-to-knee with him, holding hands. "Francesca," I breathe long and low.

The candlelight dances against my eyelids. I catch a faint whiff of feet, suppress a giggle and inhale deeply. "Francesca." The image of the hanged woman fills my mind. An airy voice moans behind my ears. I open my eyes to see Burt's reaction. Nothing. The walls blur then refocus, and nothing's changed.

Burt's still chanting, and I start again, too. My lungs expand, and I get a chill from the cold locket against my breastbone. I'm in a dark tent in the mountains, my tenth birthday. Outside, Mom and Dad dance in the whistling wind. The campfire projects their shadows over the fabric of the tent. Their waltzing boots crunch the earth. The forest sings. Dad's shape is massive in his coat; the pom-pom on Mom's stocking cap flops from side to side as they turn. The fire hisses and steams, and Mom unzips the tent to climb inside.

Through closed eyelids I perceive the darkness as the

candle dies. The smoldering wick alarms my palate. A finger strums my spine. My skin tingles and I'm floating.

I inhale, exhale to call for Francesca, but no sound emerges. I hear Burt say the woman's name, and to my own terror, I answer. *"I'm here."*

I see myself cross-legged on the floor below. I watch my chest swell and contract as I drift, unmoored from my body.

"I did it for him." My mouth produces the words in a voice that is foreign yet familiar.

Burt shifts. His eyelids flutter.

I am formless and alone, powerless to wave away the cobwebs clouding my vision. I watch my fingers move against Burt's hands.

"Are you okay?" He says, his words distant like a voice across a dark lake.

I want to scream, *I am not okay.* I want to tell him to stop this, to save me before I disappear, but I have no voice. I drift like mist as my lips move on my body below me.

"He would have killed him if I told." The words tug at my thoughts.

"Ingrid?" Burt's voice wobbles.

"He said the tea would settle her."

I wonder whose hands Burt feels in his.

"And the baby." I watch myself sob. *"But who would take my word over his?"*

"Your word over whose?" Burt asks.

"Mr. Stirling believed I did it. I couldn't live like that.

But then I couldn't leave him." I see a teardrop fall from my cheek. "*I wanted him to know the truth.*"

"What is the truth?" Burt asks.

"*I tried to make him hear me,*" Francesca's words from my lips. "*Then he was gone, too. He moves farther away each day.*" Her sorrow saturates me.

"What are we supposed to do?" Burt's voice quivers.

"*Make him see the truth.*"

"How?" Burt says.

"*Before it's too late.*"

Clouds thicken before my eyes. Sounds swirl and echo. I burn like dry ice, my skin searing with excitement as my vision goes inky and shrinks to nothing.

"Ingrid?" Burt's voice comes from a long way off. "Are you okay? Ingrid?"

The floor is hard against my knee, hip, shoulder. Something nudges my elbow. Panic surges through me, and I sputter for air, eyes open, scrambling to my feet. I'm hollow and tingling. "Where am I?" I am in my room. Burt's here. We were trying to contact a ghost. Every cell in my body grieves.

"What just happened?" Burt's pale in the dark. I brush his hot fingers from my forearm. My hands find my neck. My locket chain rests where a moment before had been coarse rope. This despair isn't mine. This is not my pain.

"Say something." Burt says.

I open my mouth and out comes a nervous chuckle. The reflex overtakes me, and I shake with silent laughter. These are my arms I wrap around Burt, my throat making these sounds. But she's still in my thoughts. I feel like I've been scraped away, and underneath is a different me, someone I've known forever but somehow forgotten. I don't know which me is thinking this, which me is the real me.

"That was not normal," Burt says.

I'm drowning in emotions I can't explain, someone else's feelings manifesting through me, mingling with my own. In the center of the whirling pool, I feel a desperate desire to numb the grief, to sever myself from all feeling, or to abandon myself to them and let them dissolve me and carry me away. I am saturated with sadness, crushed beneath it, trapped and alone and consumed by the desire to end it.

"Was that Francesca?" Burt asks.

His words ground me somehow. I flex my hand, relieved when my fingers respond. My head's bubbling over with memories, passions, emotions. These sensations do not belong to me, they do not come from me, yet they're as real and painful as a fresh burn. I stare in shock at scattered shards of porcelain, a woman crumpled on the second floor landing, her dress stained and the carpet mottled red and brown. A man menaces me, demanding that I lie, threatening to destroy Mr. Stirling if I reveal our secret; I feel the desolation of surrender as I cinch the knot to my throat and kick the wooden chair to the floor.

"Nobody believes me." My voice is tiny. I'm not even sure it's my voice.

"We need to do it again," Burt's excited. "I have to get my gear."

Of course Burt doesn't understand. I don't understand. I feel like there's someone else inside me, and I've never felt so alone. I'm afraid I'm losing myself, that this is how Mom felt.

"You have to go." I lie down on my bed.

"What was it like?"

"I want to be alone," I say. And finally he says goodbye and clunks down the stairs, and the kitchen door wheezes shut.

I am tangled in fear, fighting through a thick forest raucous with birds. A woman glimmers through the moist light. She vanishes when I turn to look. She is speaking to me, but it's the sound of my own thoughts. She's asking me to help her, and I know that's what I have to do.

I'm on my way to Burt's house, partly to apologize for kicking him out last night, partly because he's the only one I can talk to about what happened, and partly to convince him to help me to figure out how to help Francesca Moss.

The quickest way to Burt's house is through the park, and I decide to pay a visit to Leo's mother's statue. Burt isn't the only one I owe an apology to, and maybe I'm thinking that if I can explain my bizarre behavior to Leo's mother, it'll somehow get through to him.

The rose garden's less enchanting without Leo, but the burbling water soothes me. Leo's face echoes through his mother's bronze eyes, and I'm palpitating. I wonder what his mother would think of mine, and what it's like to see your mother frozen in youth.

A bouquet rests against her knees, foxglove and roses, white and scarlet, and I'm a child again. Mom presses crushed foxglove to my torn knee, and my pain's fading and I want to hold her forever. Whatever Leo's reputation, my heart goes willowy at the thought of him leaving these flowers.

Burt's not sure what to say to me at first, but I'm getting pretty good at apologies, so the air between us clears up easily. We start for the Historical Society to look at old papers, gather what information we can. Last night I couldn't speak to him, but now I gush as we walk, blathering about how Francesca wants us to help her convince Judge Stirling that she didn't kill his wife. Her innocence is as obvious to me as my own name. The rest, like why she killed herself, and why she never told Judge Stirling the truth, and why she thinks I can help, are mysteries.

"Why don't you channel Judge Stirling," Burt said. "Tell him yourself?"

"Why would he believe me?" It was bad enough to have a dead woman in my head, controlling my body. The thought of inviting possession by a man creeps me out. "First we need proof."

"Do you think we could summon them both?" Burt said. "Have them talk it out?"

I'm annoyed that he says "we," like he had anything to do with it. "Invite," I say. "Not summon." And I don't even know if it's possible, what Burt's suggesting, and I am terrified of the idea of adding yet another set of memories to my own, and even more so that I'm even asking myself these questions. "And we need to get the facts first."

"Maybe Francesca loved him? What if—"

"It wasn't that." I shake my head, surprised at the certainty.

He hits my shoulder to remind me to turn at the walkway to the WHS. "How can you be so sure?"

"I just know."

"Can't you at least try to describe it?"

"Maybe one day."

"Why not now?"

"Because now," I pull the door to the WHS, breathing

in the old-book smell, "I'm working on a 'history project.'"

The Warwick Historical Society keeps its newspaper archives in the basement. It's cool and dry, and the metal stacks glow blue under the fluorescents. Burt runs his finger along the over-sized red spines embossed with "Warwick Advertiser" in worn gold leaf. He pulls a volume from nineteen sixty-five.

The March twenty-second headline reads "City Attorney's Wife Found Dead." The article describes how the Stirlings' maid, Francesca Moss, discovered Mrs. Stirling's body. The story develops over several days. Doctor Ezra Sanford's autopsy determines the cause of death to be internal asphyxiation from cyanide poisoning. Detectives find cyanide in Mrs. Stirling's tea, and Francesca admits she prepared the tea. Despite her confession, Mr. Stirling insists Francesca stay at Mr. Stirling's home, under house arrest, confined to her room pending trial. On the morning of opening arguments, a deputy arrives to escort Francesca to the courthouse. He finds her door locked from the inside. They break it down and find her dead, hanging by her neck from the rafters.

"She was nineteen," Burt says.

The rope scratches and burns as it strangles. It's Francesca's memory, but it's as real as it is wretched.

"Why would Judge Stirling let her stay at his house?" I feel Francesca's affection for Mr. Stirling, but I don't think it's romantic. Then again, maybe I just can't recognize romance.

Burt turns a page. "They were practically siblings."

"Mr. Stirling and Francesca?"

"Sure," Burt says. "Francesca moved in when they were kids."

"She grew up there?" I don't know why this bothers me.

"Francesca's aunt was the maid for Judge Stirling's parents. Francesca lived with them in her aunt's room. When the Judge took over the house, Francesca's aunt retired, and Francesca took her place."

I admit to Burt that Francesca has strong feelings for Mr. Stirling.

"You think she killed Mrs. Stirling because she was jealous?"

"I don't think Francesca killed her at all."

"Why would she hang herself if she wasn't guilty?"

"Why would she admit to giving her the tea if she was?"

I turn another page, and my skin prickles at a photograph. The header reads, "Murderess, Suicide, Buried at Warwick Cemetery," and Francesca Moss's dark eyes stare out from the past. Lush waves of hair frame a delicate smile, so unlike the wan, lifeless face seared into my mind.

Francesca's laughing in the photo, but I can't imagine her happy. Where was that joy when she tightened the cord around her throat and stepped into eternity? What did she look like in her casket? Had they painted her face like they painted Mom, ghoulish in her flowered dress? Had they even bothered to try to make her look nice, Francesca Moss, murderess, suicide?

I want to shred the articles. I want to erase the labels they pinned onto Francesca, defining her forever by her final act, just as Mom became Isabella Bruni Van Hooten, suicide, her legacy poisoned along with her body. I want to wash away the stain on Francesca's memory. I ache with the fear that one day I'll be defined by my last moment, that anything good I do in my life will be overshadowed by one moment of weakness. I'm afraid of the fear that drove Francesca to hang herself, and I recognize the source of her fear. "It was Dr. Sanford," I say, not knowing how I know, only that his name on my lips drains me of hope.

It takes Burt a moment before he gets my meaning. "Why would Dr. Sanford kill Mrs. Stirling?"

"I don't know," I say. "But Francesca isn't lying. She might be wrong, but she believes she's telling the truth."

"Lucky for us, he's dead, too."

"How is that lucky?" I ask.

"That means we don't have to accuse Leo's uncle of murder."

My anxiety returns in force, and I'm angry at myself for not considering that this affects Leo, too. I know how it feels for people to label Mom a suicide. How much worse would it be to find out the man who raised you was a murderer?

"There's no reason to tell Leo."

"I'm all for that."

"It's not like we have to put Dr. Sanford on trial or anything." I'm justifying the secret. "The only person we have to convince is Judge Stirling." But we have no proof. It's still just thoughts in my head. I'm not sure I would believe anyone who claimed to know something because they'd been possessed by a ghost.

"Maybe someone around remembers more."

chapter eleven

Burt and I pick our way along a creek to find a man Burt says was involved in the murder investigation. The heat has relented, and the air has a clean, dry warmth in the shade of a magnificent stand of oaks. I wonder how much water has passed beneath their branches.

The back of Burt's hand grazes mine, but I ignore it.

"Are you all right?" he asks.

"Sure." Seeing the photograph of Francesca has relieved me in a way, confirming she's more than just a fabrication of my mind.

"You don't look so great."

"You're a real peach."

"I mean you looked kind of sick back there."

"I feel like I'm sharing my head with a long-lost twin."

"Kindred spirits."

"You're hilarious," I punch his arm, not hard. "We're both separated from our parents. We're both misunderstood."

"You're both beautiful."

I let the compliment sparkle in the air.

"In an exotic sort of way."

"We both live in the same house, in the same room."

"Live?"

I'm about to ask him what he means when he stops me and points. "There's our guy."

Chief Waldman reclines in a folding chair on a gravel flat beside the creek. A bucket and cooler sit beside him, and a fishing pole leans in a stand. The line is slack in the brown water, and he's reading a hardback book.

"Mr. Waldman?" Burt calls from a polite distance.

The trees stir, and their shadows sway over the water. The man closes his book over his thumb and turns to us. A white smear of sunscreen adorns his bald skull. "Can I help you?"

"Are you Mr. Waldman?" Burt asks.

"Chief."

"We were wondering if we could bother you with a few questions," I say.

The man regards my hair but betrays no expression.

"It's for a history project," I say.

The creek ripples past, its surface shaped by the stones below.

"Not big on history," Chief Waldman says.

"Mr. MacLeish said you might be able to help," Burt says.

The chief turns back to the water and stretches his arms, holding the book in one hand. "Most people fish in the mornings." He stretches his legs one at a time. "Say the fish won't rise in the heat of the day."

Burt nods. I wondered if the man's being evasive or senile.

"See that pool?" He points to a shady patch of water. "There's fish in there."

"What kind of fish?" Burt asks.

"That really what you're asking?"

"Excuse me?"

"Sit down." He taps the cooler. "I can talk fishing all day."

I say, "Do you mind if we ask you about Dottie Stirling?"

"Know why I fish this time of day?" If he recognizes the name, nothing in his demeanor shows it. "No damn fishermen."

Burt's laugh sounds forced.

"You think that's funny?"

Burt flushes. "I thought you were making a joke."

"Do you remember her?" I ask. "She was murdered."

His lips curl the slightest bit. "You're new around here."

"Yes, sir."

"You know what else I like about fishing this time of day? No damn fish to interrupt me." He thumps the cover of his book.

I startle, hoping he isn't about to chase us off.

"I didn't read much when I was younger," he says, "outside of the bullshit for work."

"What are you reading now?" Burt turns his head to see

the spine.

"Whatever I want."

I find a dry patch of gravel and sit. "We we were hoping you might remember what happened. Details that might not have been in the papers."

"You know what we called people like you on the force?"

I shake my head and brace for his answer.

"Detective."

I smile in relief.

"So, have at it, detective," the chief says.

"Did Francesca Moss really do it?"

"Nope."

"Who did?"

"I meant that wasn't a very good question. A good detective doesn't give away so much."

"Who do you think killed her?"

"When you said 'really' you told me that you don't think Francesca Moss did it. Hell, the fact that you asked at all told me that, but the 'really' waved it in my face."

"What should I have asked?"

"Start broad."

"What do you mean?"

"Ask general questions. Let your subject talk, but don't let him know what you're after right away."

"What do you remember about the case?"

"Exactly." He sits forward, and I'm feeling like I'm doing a good job. "Get your subject to wander around in the facts a while, stir up his memory, and when he gets near where you want him to go, you just work him to it."

"Do you remember when Dottie Stirling died?"

"Course, it won't work now because I already know what you're after. So, here's the meat: nobody ever said where that girl got her hands on the poison, and nobody put forth any motive that held water."

"So you don't think she did it?" I feel vindicated.

"Thing was, the girl confessed."

"Why do you think she confessed?"

The chief looks to Burt. "Why are you letting her do all the work?"

Burt's voice comes out an octave higher than usual. "She's doing a good job?"

"Know what we call that?" Chief jerks a finger at Burt. "Call that a good partner. Knows when to keep his trap shut."

Burt does a poor job of hiding his grin.

"Who do you think did it?" I ask.

"Here's another lesson: when a job's done, let it be done."

"But it's not done." I say this quickly, before doubt becomes fear.

"Who am I to question that girl's confession?"

"What if it wasn't the truth?" I say.

"*Pluralitas non est ponenda sine neccesitate.*"

"But—" I begin to protest.

"Sorry?" Burt says.

"Roughly translated," the chief says, "means I had a dead girl and a live one said she killed her," delivering the words like a nurse delivers a hypodermic.

"What about justice?" I say too loud.

"My job's order."

My face must be glowing. "What if she was—"

"And nothing my guys did or didn't do could've brought that girl back."

I'm trembling angry, but his tone makes me think twice about responding.

"You know what the best part about being retired is?" The chief turns and stretches his legs again. "I get to do this." And he leans back into his chair and returns to his book.

I'm fuming as we hike back down the creek to where it feeds into the Wawayanda. Downstream, on the opposite bank, there's the bluff with the firepit. Overhead, raptors ride the thermals. Burt says, "He seems like a friendly guy."

I'm too pissed to laugh at his sarcasm. "He's a coward." I slip on the wet stones but stay on my feet. "Afraid to confront the mighty Dr. Sanford."

"He was pretty powerful," Burt says. "And Francesca did confess."

I have no time for this. "She admitted giving her the tea, not poisoning it," I say, speeding up.

"Killing herself didn't exactly scream 'innocent.'"

"I—She didn't do it!"

"Slow down." Burt's breathing heavy behind me.

"I can't. We're running out of time."

"What does that mean?" he says.

"We have to hurry," I say. I don't know why, but it's true. "Time's running out."

"Maybe the reason she wants to contact Judge Stirling," Burt says, "isn't because she's innocent. Maybe she just wants to apologize."

It's all I can do not to pick up a rock and smash his head. "She's not guilty!"

He makes a sound, affirmative but skeptical.

"I know she didn't do it."

"How can you be so sure?" Burt says, and I feel the trap close around me.

"She's in my head." I shouldn't have said it.

"Maybe she's delusional? What if she believes her own lie?"

I'm running now, away from Burt and away from the idea that Francesca might believe a lie, that a person can trick herself like that. I've seen firsthand what happens to someone who can't tell reality from fantasy. I hit a patch of mud and go down. My head bounces hard off the ground and light fills my eyes. The world comes back into focus. I'm inches away from the water. Insects skate on the tension.

Burt splashes in, and the insects scatter. He helps me

up. I brush mud from my cheek, and the pain in my head fades. Nothing seems too damaged, but I take it slow as we walk together. "If Francesca killed Mrs. Stirling," I say, "why would Mr. Stirling let her stay at his house?"

"He didn't think she'd be safe in jail," Burt says. "He didn't want anything interfering with her trial."

"He believed she did it?" I know this already. I've known it since she possessed me. But I'm disappointed beyond explanation.

"He trusted the system."

We climb up out of the river bed, and I don't know where we are. "He should have trusted me." I catch myself. "I mean 'her.'" The feelings that surround this are confused: part of me understands Mr. Stirling's anger, and part of me feels betrayed, but mostly I'm terrified. Of what, or of whom, I don't know.

Burt says. "How certain are you that Dr. Sanford did it?"

The source of my fear becomes instantly obvious. "Certain."

Burt won't look at me. He blinks and gulps air. He's resisting something, but finally he says, "I have an idea."

I raise my eyebrows, waiting.

"Promise you won't freak out?"

"Speak."

"I think we should summon her again."

"I can't believe you—"

"We could record it."

"You want to record me being possessed."

"We can show the police."

"You want me to be committed?"

"You said you wouldn't freak out."

"First of all," I fight for calm. "If they didn't care about the truth forty years ago, why would they start now? Second of all, we don't have time to wait for some investigation. And third of all," I'm quivering with anger, "are you seriously asking me to go on camera claiming to be possessed by a woman who was accused of murder and killed herself?"

"I thought maybe ... "

"That you might use the recording to show up those guys from GHAST." I'm practically spitting. "Not even thinking about what happens to me?"

He opens his mouth but I cut him off.

"My dad will be like, 'Why were we worried about Ingrid? There's nothing at all crazy about my daughter claiming to be possessed by a woman who killed herself forty years ago.'"

"Fine, I—"

"It'll take the Witch about six seconds to get me into a straitjacket."

"You're right," he raises his hands in surrender. "I didn't think it through."

"You thought it through for yourself!" I'm yelling, "Not for me."

His silence seems sincere, as if he realizes his mistake. But I walk away anyway. I feel victorious, and it sucks. As angry as I am at Burt, I'm also glad when he follows me and finally breaks the silence.

"Maybe there's something in the medical records," he says.

"I didn't see a 'medical records' section at the Historical Society."

"Dr. Sanford's clinic," Burt says. "He saw his regular patients in the clinic in Leo's house."

"Why would he keep her files for so long?"

"He was a scientist. He'd sooner cut off his own finger than lose a scrap of data. And Leo hasn't let anyone inside the clinic since his uncle died."

"Can you get us inside?" I ask.

"I'm sure Leo'd let you in."

"No way am I asking Leo to dig around his house so I can prove his uncle was a murderer." I let this sink in. "But I hear you're pretty good at getting into places without permission."

"What's that supposed to mean?"

"I heard something about an old hospital or something."

"Did you also hear I'm on probation because of it?"

"Then we both have something to lose."

145

chapter twelve

A sickle moon hangs over the deserted streets. Burt digs out two pairs of gloves and hands one to me. A sign hangs bolted from the side of Sanford House: "Ezra Sanford, MD, Patients please use front entrance" spelled out in cursive.

Burt unrolls a leather pouch filled with what look like dental tools. He works the slender picks into the deadbolt slot, and in a few seconds the clinic door opens. This isn't the most frightened I've ever been, but it's the most frightened I've been on purpose.

Then he takes a pair of flashlights from his pack. "Keep the light off the windows," he whispers as we creep through a small break-room then into the clinic itself. His beam crosses a row of curtained examination rooms on the far wall. A pair of long black tables occupies the center of the room. The light falls over a microscope covered in clear plastic, metal racks of dusty flasks and beakers, a handful of microwave-sized machines.

My hands quiver, and I'm relying on Burt's confidence as he directs me to a row of cabinets while he moves down a hall towards what I think is the front of the house. After a minute, his whisper crosses the darkness. "In here."

I follow his voice into a large, windowless room filled with metal shelves and file cabinets. Burt skims the stacks, and I scan drawers until I come to one marked "S." I ease the drawer open and finger through the tabs. "Burt," I say, my whisper is loud in the quiet dark.

"What is it?" Burt says.

"Mrs. Stirling's file." I page through forms and charts, the taste of stale carbon ink on my lips.

Burt stops my hand. He reaches in and pulls a form marked "Paternity Test/Amniocentesis." A table of columns: genotypes, alleles, and strings of letters and numbers ends with a short paragraph at the bottom. "Test completed March 20, 1965, seventy-six days into term, confirms Specimen 766349667 is not excluded as the biological father of subject unborn child."

"This is two days before—" I stop at the unmistakable sound of a key in a lock. My heart thumps against my ribs. I'm breathing like a horse.

Burt's light vanishes. "Shhh." He slides the file into his pack.

I switch off my light, not knowing whether to hide or flee. Burt pulls me to the floor.

Heavy footsteps thud through the clinic. A wide, white beam glares across the open door to the file room.

We creep on hands and knees, feeling our way deeper into the room.

A figure moves past the door. The front entrance to the clinic rattles, then the light flashes past again. I'm holding my breath. The figure stops in the door. The flashlight illuminates one corner, then another, shining over our heads. Pressed to the floor, I try to quiet my thumping heart. I'm trembling, afraid to look. I smell Burt's sweat, feel his moist hand covering mine, and I'm begging in my head "please leave please leave please." The beam crosses the room again, again too high to spot us. I allow in the thinnest stream of air, but the sound rushes in my ears like a storm.

The overheads flicker on.

"Hold it right there," a man shouts.

I hide my face.

"Hands where I can see them."

I open my eyes to see a midnight blue uniform. Cold metal ratchets into my wrists. I turn to Burt, chewing his lip as the policeman radios in.

chapter thirteen

The holding cell is three walls of olive tile, a steel ledge bolted to the back wall for sitting, and a fourth wall of steel bars. Camera domes watch from the ceiling.

I perch on the ledge in a corner. My feet bounce of their own accord. Burt leans on his knees, staring out the bars where an expressionless woman watches a console full of screens.

Outside of the cage, beyond the console, glass doors seal our cell from the main station. Policemen move inaudibly beyond the glass, their polished belts heavy with equipment. The station shimmers with electronics and screens, looking like a cross between the trading floor at Dad's office and the command center of a spaceship.

I hug my trembling self to keep from bursting into tears.

The console chirps, and the woman says, "Send him in."

The glass doors sweep open, bringing the murmur of the busy station and Leo Sanford, dangling Burt's backpack.

Burt leaps to his feet. "Get us out of here." Burt grips the bars in front of Leo.

"Home invasion, Giles? I thought you preferred ceme-teries and asylums?"

"Can you gloat later?" Burt asks.

"I'm curious why my so-called friends would be breaking into my house."

"I can explain," Burt says.

I wonder what, exactly, he would tell Leo.

"Let us out," Burt says.

"In due time," Leo says, then turns to me. "Did he tell you my house was haunted?"

"Please tell them it's all a mistake," I say.

Leo signals to the woman at the console. A buzzer sounds, the bars slide open, and Leo walks through. "I do get some small measure of joy at seeing you in your native habitat," he says to Burt. "But it kills me to think of this beautiful creature caged."

I'm stress-acned and crumbling, but when his finger raises my chin and my eyes meet his, I'm soaring.

"Don't be afraid," he says, and I fight to keep my face impassive.

"Quit the theatrics," Burt says. "And tell them we weren't trespassing."

"Not so fast." Leo turns to Burt. "Freedom, as they say, isn't free."

"Sergeant Watkins," Leo calls to the policewoman. "May I please have a moment alone with the suspects?" The sergeant slips out of her headset. The glass doors whoosh open then shut behind her.

"As confused as I am about why two of my most intimate confidantes would invade my home," he unzips Burt's backpack, "I'm positively baffled that you stole this?" He brandishes Mrs. Stirling's medical file.

"Get to the point," Burt says.

"My point, Giles, is that this is your lucky day." He claps his hand on Burt's shoulder. "I need your help."

"With what?"

"Just say yes."

"Why should I?"

"Why should I tell the police this is all a misunderstanding?"

"What do you want?"

"Not here." He nods at a camera. "Why don't I give you two a ride home?"

"Thanks," I say.

Burt narrows his eyes. "We can get home on our own."

"I guess it's just us, then," Leo offers me his hand. I wipe fingerprint solution onto my jeans and take it. His fingers are soft and strong.

He escorts me out and presses a button on the console. The cage clangs shut.

"You're leaving him?"

"Bye, Burt," Leo says. "Keep in mind that tampering with medical records is a federal crime." A second button opens the glass doors.

151

"You can't." I stop.

"It's his choice."

"Burt, please," I say. "I need you."

Leo drops my hand. "Ouch."

"Open the cell," I say.

"Anyone I can call for you?" Leo says to Burt. "Your probation officer, perhaps?"

"Fine, I'll help you," Burt says, and Leo opens the cage.

In the parking lot, Leo opens the passenger door of a low-slung convertible and pushes the seat forward and gestures for Burt to squeeze into the back. I take the shotgun seat, and when Leo ignites the throaty engine, all I can think of is exhaust and ventilation.

Leo pushes the car hard. I'm still jangly from the arrest, but when Leo accelerates into a tight curve, I'm clenching my seatbelt and bracing my feet against the floor.

We rocket through a forest, climbing up into the mountains. My stomach flips when we burst out of the tunnel of trees onto an open ridge, the valley falling away. The mountains creep along the horizon, and infinite stars speckle the sky.

I don't recognize the route, and Burt confirms my suspicion. "Where're we going?" he yells over the wind.

"To get some perspective," Leo shouts back.

We plunge back into thick forest. Leo downshifts, and I lurch forward as the car settles onto the shoulder. Leo cuts the engine. My breathing's loud with confusion and relief, and the only other sound is the drone of insects.

"Come on." Leo strides into the woods, swinging Burt's backpack.

I step out, and Burt unfolds from the back. "What are we doing?" he asks, trotting behind Leo into the dark.

If there's a path, it's invisible to me. I stumble over roots. Branches claw at my arms, still tender from the hollies. The air's thick with bitter pine.

Finally we come out of the woods and Leo's silhouetted against a curtain of stars. Far below, cradled among the hills, the village sparkles. I look down and realize that one more step and I'm falling, dead in a blink. I lower myself to the rocks and make myself small against the gusting wind. Puffs of clouds glow as they pass.

"Be careful." Burt's beside us.

My heart's galloping, and I swallow hard and try not to think about falling.

"Isn't it beautiful?" Leo says.

In the distant village, far below us, pinpoints of street lamps outline the square, and the black void of the river snakes through the lights of the town. Headstones wink in the cemetery, and one polished side of the Sanford pyramid glows with reflected starlight. The way the village melds into the forest and hills stirs something poignant, like it's some precious thing I want to preserve, but it's too large and too grand to even comprehend.

"My great-great-great-grandfather could've settled anywhere," Leo says. "But he wanted to immerse himself in the purity of the wilderness, to build a community where men celebrated the highest elements of civilization."

"Too bad it ended up being this dump," Burt says.

"Don't be so jaded," Leo replies. "We have clean streets and excellent schools. We'll marry our high school sweethearts, have healthy children in our cutting-edge hospital, and raise them in our perfect little town."

"Cut the tourist crap," Burt says.

"It's nice to hear someone proud of his home," I say.

"It's easy for him," Burt says. "He owns it all."

"Just because I have a big stake," Leo says, "doesn't mean it's easy."

"Tell us how hard it is," Burt hurls a rock into the darkness. "And while you're at it, explain what we're doing up here."

"You explain why you broke into my uncle's clinic!" A flurry of wind accompanies Leo's outburst. "I know he put you up to this," he yells at me. "What did he tell you you'd find?"

"Leave her alone," Burt's on his feet now, between Leo and me. "She doesn't have to tell you anything."

"Why were you stealing medical records?"

I want to tell him everything, how I'm trying to help

Francesca, how we snuck in to protect Leo from the truth about his uncle, not steal.

"I should've left you in jail." Leo shoves, and Burt stumbles backwards.

"Cut it out!" I lunge for Burt, but he lands on his back and slides down the rock headfirst. He stops short of the edge, and a small avalanche of debris skitters down the rockface in warning.

"Who is Dorothy Stirling?" Leo shakes the file folder in his fist.

"It's about your uncle," Burt says.

"What about him?"

"He did something awful," Burt says.

"It has nothing to do with you," I say.

"And this," Leo strikes a lighter. The flash turns my vision to spots, but the flame doesn't take, "has nothing to do with you."

"Why do you even care?" Burt asks. "You hated your uncle."

"You don't know what you're talking about," Leo says. His lighter catches on the second try, and a blue flame hisses for a second before the wind extinguishes it. "He hated me." The wind lulls, and Leo snaps the lighter again. The flame holds, its tongue licking the dry folder.

Burt's glowing face shows no expression. It kills me to watch my best hope for proving Francesca's innocence curl and blacken and lift into the air. I can't tell if it's my heart or Francesca's that's breaking. Leo releases the final scrap of flaming paper to the sky.

"Can we go home now?" Burt says when it's done.

"Can we?" Leo mocks.

"You're right," the words leap from my mouth. "This is beautiful." I gesture to the panorama. "And I appreciate you getting us out of jail. And I'm sorry about breaking in. But, please, if I don't get home before my grandparents wake up, they'll ship me off to rehab."

"I can't let that happen," Leo smiles. Even in the darkness, his eyes sparkle. "But Burt still owes me a favor."

Burt sighs.

"I have a package arriving from Toronto. I need you to fetch it for me."

"I'm not going to Canada."

"Tomorrow, ten p.m. The bus leaves at noon."

"What am I supposed to tell my parents?" Burt says.

"Couldn't care less." Leo starts back to the car.

"What's in the package?" Burt and I follow.

"Use your imagination."

"I could get arrested."

"I could take you to jail right now." Leo holds the handle of the car door. "Do this, and we'll wipe the slate clean."

I hate myself for wanting Burt to give in, and when he agrees and Leo starts the car, relief starts to settle in. But as we drive all I can think about is Leo burning that file then blackmailing Burt into going on some shady errand, so by the time Leo drops Burt and parks by my house, my relief has morphed into anger.

I open the car door without a word, and I'm frustrated because even though I'm pissed at Leo, I also don't want him to go. So I just sit there like a dope, waiting for him to apologize or, if not, then at least say something that'll make me just flat-out hate him.

"It's nothing bad, you know." He finally says. "Burt's little trip." I want to believe him, but picturing Burt meeting some drug dealer, crossing an international border, makes me shudder.

"What do you have against him?"

"Nothing, really." He leans against his car and buries his hands in his pockets. "It's just that every time we're together, he seems to show up."

I should be ashamed at how easy it is for him to redeem himself, but my heart is singing. He wants to be with me. "I'm sorry about the other morning." I went out like a basket case, but he's still interested. "That wasn't the real me."

"You didn't seem yourself." His smile defuses my embarrassment. "Let's hang out tomorrow night," he says. "While Burt's safe on a bus."

My head's a maelstrom of ghosts and handcuffs and murder and routine and rules and the GALS embargo and the possibility of love and the fact that I can't hide my stupid grin.

"I'd like to ... " I silently curse Dr. Spangler's rules. If it's a friends date, then maybe it's okay. "But ... " But I don't want it to be a friends date.

He scrunches his eyes like someone preparing for something unpleasant.

"I'm not supposed to date right now."

"Who says?"

I want to tell him the truth, but I can't bear to poison whatever is growing between us with the "I might be crazy or just traumatized by my mother's suicide" conversation, so I lie.

"I can't date a drug dealer." My stomach sinks because I realize how badly I want to go out with him, and how this excuse that I thought just came to me actually is a deal-breaker.

He's rolling his eyes and smiling like this is nothing, but I'm serious.

"I needed the money."

"You realize how ridiculous that sounds?"

"Ironic, I know. But for my uncle, the purse strings were just another tool for him to control me. It was nice to have some of my own."

"But you're still doing it."

"Sort of," he says. "As a favor for the guys. I don't even charge them."

He spins crime into altruism. But I'm going to have to tell Dr. Spangler, so I have to press my luck. "Would you give it up?" I'm a nag even before we start. "For me?"

"Done."

I'm willing to believe him. "Then I guess that just leaves my grandparents."

"I'll ask them tomorrow."

So it's out of my hands. And if Grandma agrees, it would have to be all right.

chapter fourteen

I get up on time and drag my exhausted body through my morning routine. I try to nap, but the pounding of the renovation is too much. I write a few sentences about my grandparents' new house and the drama of its former occupants, but really I'm fighting the growing anxiety that if I don't help Francesca soon, I never will. And, as if there's any other space in my head, I'm imagining the conversation that's about to take place between Leo and Grandma.

I take up my journal, hoping to brainstorm ways to find evidence of Francesca's innocence. There's only one reason for a paternity test. Dr. Sanford knew who the father was, and the fact that paternity was in question has to be related to the poisoning. Who else knew? Stirling? Whoever the other candidate for father was? I wonder if Mrs. Stirling's death was a mistake. I wonder if she was trying to abort the pregnancy.

My thoughts swirl but come to no conclusions. And I keep spinning back to Leo setting fire to the only tangible clue that might help Francesca. I want to hate him for it, but I also want to understand why he did it.

I can't believe Leo is as bad as the girls said. He rescued me last night. He left flowers by his mother's statue. He's kind of a jerk to Burt, but he did that to spend time with me. It doesn't hurt that he's outwardly heavenly. And what more proof of his sincerity than the fact that he still likes me after my lunacy in the garden. I weigh the date with Leo against my friendship with Angel and Heather, maybe Burt, too, and I realize that if Grandma says yes, I'm going to break the embargo. And I'm doodling "Ingrid Van Hooten Sanford" in fancy script when a knock at the front door launches a jolt of excitement.

I smooth my hair and force myself to take the steps one at a time. I round the bend into the foyer, and there's Grandpa, but instead of Leo, it's Burt, rocking from foot to foot.

"I wanted to ask you a favor," Burt says to me.

I look at Grandpa, who, after a long second, excuses himself.

"What happened last night?" He asks.

I'm afraid he knows Leo asked me out. "What do you mean?"

"Did you see her?"

I check for grandparents and shake my head, a finger on my lips.

"Take this," Burt holds his handheld recorder for me.

I don't move to take the device. "What am I supposed to do with that?"

"Set it up in your room tonight, in case she shows up again."

"We tried that already."

"You want proof, don't you?"

"I want proof Francesca's innocent," I whisper.

"Without proof she's real, they'll think you're crazy." I pray no one can hear this.

The device is warm from his hand, small enough to fit in a pocket. "Recording myself sleep isn't crazy?"

"Just keep it with you. If we actually record a ghost, it'll be epic."

"We?"

"And stay away from Leo."

"Why would you say that?" I look over Burt's shoulder, hoping not to see Leo coming.

"He's setting me up."

"I'm sure it's nothing."

"Why are you defending him?"

"I'm sure you'll be fine," I say in a hushed voice.

"And what about you?"

"I think I'll survive," I say.

"Let's hope I do, too." He says, doing some weird half-wave thing with both hands like he's angling in for a goodbye hug. I pretend not to notice for an awkward moment until he gives up and leaves.

Burt isn't gone ten minutes before Leo shows, blue eyes sparkling and his smile in full force as he greets Grandma and me through the screen.

"Hello." Grandma's smile is a welcome surprise. "Don't leave your friend standing outside," she tells me.

The three of us crowd into the foyer, between the plastic-curtained doorways and the boxes. The workers must be at lunch, because the house is quiet. "Won't you stay?" Grandma asks. "I've just made fresh lemonade."

"Thank you, but I can't," Leo says. "I only stopped by to see if Ingrid wanted to go to a school function this evening."

"Tell me about this function."

I'm trying to hide my excitement, but I feel a little like property they're haggling over.

"It's a cookout for the rising seniors."

"A chaperoned event?"

"Of course." He makes the least sincere guffaw ever.

"She'll be home by nine?"

"Absolutely." He doesn't blink at the pre-dark curfew.

"I'll check with Ingrid's grandfather," Grandma excuses herself, and we're alone, and my heart quickens when I realize how close he is to me.

"Did you get any sleep?" Leo asks.

"Barely," I press my knuckles to the bags under my eyes. "I must look hideous."

"You look great."

"Burt's freaking out."

Leo laughs through his nose, and I immediately regret letting on I've talked to Burt. "Of course he is." There's an element of cruelty to his tone, but I tell myself it's just a friendly joke.

Grandma makes a big production of clomping back through the kitchen. I put on my innocent-but-enthusiastic face. Grandma says okay, and that's that. Fate had settled it. GALS be damned. And I haven't had to decide anything.

I'm ready long before Leo knocks, but I play it cool, listening from upstairs while he chats up my grandparents. Finally Grandpa calls for me.

I check the mirror again, and I'm second-guessing the eyeliner and blush, slight as it is. I haven't worn makeup in forever. What if I overdid it? But it's too late now, so I pocket my lip gloss and try to find a casual stride.

Grandma, Grandpa and Leo all watch my descent. I couldn't be more self-conscious.

"Don't you look cute," Grandma says.

Puppies are cute.

She's holding a bouquet of scarlet roses. "Leo was telling us about his family's gardens."

My stomach drops, but I try to play it off. "I'd like to see them some time."

Leo jumps in, "Your grandfather tells me you've been

helping him with the planting here, too."

"A little," I say, just wanting to leave.

"Nothing like roots in the ground," Grandpa claps me on the shoulder. "To make a place feel like home."

"Should we go?" I look to Leo.

"The place is looking much better," Leo says. I imagine how bad it must have been for this to be an improvement.

"You'll hardly recognize it before long," says Grandpa.

"We'll have a brand-new bedroom for Ingrid," Grandma says. "And we're hoping she'll stay beyond the summer."

It's the first I've heard of this, and as annoying as it is to be put on the spot, I don't object.

Then, like a conversational escape artist, he says, "It was a pleasure to talk with you Mrs. Bruni, Mr. Bruni," and, still pumping Grandpa's hand, opens the door for me.

"Hope you don't get rained out," Grandpa raises his farmer's eye to the sky.

"Who else will be at this party?" I ask, resisting the urge to take his arm as we walk to the street.

"Nobody." Leo scoops up a backpack from behind a tree.

"What's in there?" I glance back at the porch, empty.

"Dinner."

"I thought we were going to your school thing?"

"I have a better idea," he says. "If it's okay with you."

He lied to my grandparents so I didn't have to. I'll have to finesse the conversation when I get home, maybe even tell the truth. I'm sixteen, after all, and I'll keep their ridiculously early curfew. "Sure."

I feel feathery, but my lightness is weighed down by a nagging guilt about Burt, chewing his nails on the bus. I remind myself that he's not really in danger, and that if he weren't on that bus, I wouldn't be here with Leo. And, as helpful as he tries to be, he really only likes to talk about ghosts. Leo, on the other hand, actually asks about me: my history report (I joke that it might never get done, mainly because I don't want to talk to Leo about Mrs. Stirling), my life in the city (carefully omit all the bad stuff), my favorite bands (I realize my playlist is all pre-Mom).

At the square, part of me's on alert for anyone who might report my whereabouts to my grandparents. But I'm a responsible girl, and I'm entitled to change my mind about where I go.

Leo's undeterred by my vague answers, and I'm glad when he turns back to gardening. Finally something I can talk about without sounding like a total head case. I show him the hard-earned blisters.

"Mother would approve," he says.

"She was a gardener?" I almost add "too" because I want his mom to like mine.

"The roses were her specialty," Leo says. "Uncle Ezra

managed the rest."

"The guy whose book you won't let me read."

"You can read whatever you like," he says. "I just said not to believe it."

"Was he really so bad?"

"He was ... " he searches for the word and finally settles on "a perfectionist."

I'm wondering how I can work this back to Francesca, but Leo goes on.

"Those bonsai, for example. He was obsessed with training them, getting closer and closer to perfection."

"How perfect can a tree be," I ask, "when it's stuck in a pot?"

"Uncle Ezra believed in the perfect tree."

"Perfect for what?" I say. "Decoration? Carbon sequestration?"

"Just perfect," he says. "Capital 'P.'"

The treetops twist, and a gust shivers through the leaves.

"Do you think there's really such thing as a capital-P-Perfect tree?" I can't help but notice the oaks towering over us as we cross the square. "How would it compare to a capital-N-Normal Tree?"

"A fair question," he says.

"Is there such a thing as a Perfect anything?"

"This might be a Perfect Date?"

Charming, but the GALS warned me about this.

"Are you one, too," I ask, "a perfectionist?"

"It's in my blood," he says, and then, in a deep voice, with an officious accent, "'Sanford's don't settle for A-minuses.'"

His impersonation is ridiculous yet appealing.

"Seriously." Leo says. "My uncle said that kind of stuff every day."

As much as I need to learn more about his uncle, I can't bring myself to do it. So I just enjoy walking beside him, wishing he'd take my hand, wondering what would happen if I took his.

The wind is pulling the clouds together, and even though it's early, it's getting dark. We leave the square, crossing the street toward the Town Hall with its tall clock tower, and Leo's house on the hill behind it. His house is dark, too, and I wonder what I'll say if that's our destination. Leo takes my hand, and I'm letting myself believe he heard me wish for this. He leads me around to the back of the Town Hall. He descends a stairwell, looks dramatically over each shoulder, and, with a magician's flourish, produces a key.

"Are we allowed to be here?"

The directionless glow of dusk is enough to make our way through the basement and up a staircase to a marble entrance hall. Every breath echoes in the polished emptiness.

"Don't worry," Leo points to a set of ornate wooden doors. "Everyone's gone for the night."

Another staircase takes us to the second floor. I'm listening for footsteps, and we pass an open courtroom, dread shivers through me. I see it with Francesca's eyes, and phantom shackles bind my wrists. I look for Leroy Stirling, not at his usual seat at the prosecutor's table, but in the gallery with the rest of the town assembled to watch my conviction.

On the third floor, we enter a storage room. Leo unfolds a ladder beneath a hatch in the ceiling and waves for me to climb.

"After you," I say and straighten the hem of my skirt.

He goes up first and helps me through the hatch, and we're in the tower, behind the clock. The remaining three sides are open, and brick arches support the roof. Through the clockworks, the backwards twelve is as high as Leo's head. People bustle through the town square, propelled by the electricity of the coming storm.

The enormous clock's second hand winds backwards. Turning around, I'm faced with Sanford House, its windows glistening like moist eyes. Beyond the mansion the clouds have decapitated the mountains. Seconds escape with insistent tocks. The groan of the twisting trees crescendos and falls.

Leo twists open a bottle. I'm relieved its sparkling lemonade.

"This is incredible," I say it loud over the wind, blasting waves through the treetops as it rolls down the mountains.

Leo's shoulder presses against mine. "My great-grand-father donated these forests as a preserve." I detect pride in his voice. "He wanted to surround the village with wilderness."

The air rumbles. A flash illuminates a cloud bank, and I see forlorn faces in the swirling moisture. A thunderclap rattles my chest, and I clutch Leo's arm.

"We're perfectly safe," he says.

"We used to love storms, Mom and I." I hesitate to invoke her, but I'm surprised at how good it feels. "We'd go out onto the pier." I hold my whipping hair from my eyes. "Dad would shout at us to come inside, insisting we'd be struck by lightning." I feel Mom coming alive in my words. "She'd twirl me, my feet flying in the wind, cool rain on our faces."

"Storms remind me of my parents, too." His words are dark as the sky.

"How old were you?" I say, trying to keep my voice impassive, as if I'm a veteran, hardened against death.

"I was eleven when they drowned."

I search for words, but they're all too flimsy. I take his hand and watch the sky.

"It felt like the world died with them," he says to the distance, but I feel us growing closer, like his words are weaving us together.

"Without them," he says, "it's like none of this is real."

He speaks without a hint of self-consciousness. The

forest twists and trembles in a violent gust. Lightning etches the sky, and a sound like ripping metal shakes me. "What about me?" I imagine a bolt striking the tower, the two of us visible to the bones, our flesh seared, our bodies fused. "Is this real?"

Leo only stares.

I flinch at another burst of thunder, and I'm a child again, squealing in Mom's arms, her hair weeping rain. I dare to ask, "Do you ever feel like they're still with you?"

"I want to."

"I think about Mom every day." The storm inhales, and in the brief stillness, the air softens. "I'd give anything to go back to the way it was. But I'll always know how it ends."

"How'd she die?"

I love him for not knowing, for not being afraid of it.

"She killed herself."

Leo nods but won't look at me.

"Don't feel bad," I say. "Nobody knows what to say." The sad truth is, he's the first to ask.

"How can I not feel bad," he says to the sky. "Knowing your own mother would do that to you."

Not even Dr. Spangler would have dared. His words stab, like he's carving something rotten out of me. I'd rather hurl myself from the tower rather than agree with him.

The first fat drop thunks onto the roof. A second later it's bucketing down, and the wind's driving the rain through our shelter.

"What would you say," he asks, "if you could go back and see her?"

"I couldn't." I'm back on the wheel of sadness and anger and guilt and sadness. "I'm afraid—" I choke on the words and try again. "I'm afraid of what I'd say."

I hear my own words through Francesca's ears, and I wonder if she feels the ache of Mom's suicide. I wonder if Mom feels my own pain, and I'm hoping she does, so I can hurt her the way she hurt me. I hate myself for wanting this.

I bury my face in Leo's chest, and I can't stop crying. I'm too exposed. I'm giving away too much. I don't know him enough to share like this. But he's not running away. He just holds on to me. The mountains have vanished. The square is empty, and the gushing rain is the only sound in our world.

"I'm sorry," I say. I look up at him. Water drips off his nose. "Do you want to go?"

"No."

We hold each other while the rain subsides. It's still gray, but the mountains reappear through the mist.

"You must think I'm bats." I say

"Who wouldn't be?" He shrugs, "after that." I wish he'd just said "no."

"How's the rest of your family holding up?" Leo asks.

"Grandma took it pretty hard," I say, and with the words comes fresh guilt. "Other than her and Grandpa, it's just Dad and me." I justify not knowing how Dad feels by reminding myself it took him all of four months to remarry. He said I needed a female role model. That lie still turns my stomach. "Dad's not much of a sharer."

"Sounds like my uncle," Leo says. The mention of Dr. Sanford stirs terror and rage. These are not my emotions, and for a moment I hope these memories and feelings are just symptoms of my malfunctioning mind. I'd rather be insane than have Leo be related to that man.

Leo kicks the lemonade bottle, sending it clanking across the wet roof. "Uncle Ezra's favorite topic was how much of a failure I am."

"You don't seem like a failure to me." My face warms. I'm no good at flattery.

"Lazy and spoiled," he says. He yanks the soggy blanket from under the picnic, scattering the tins holding down the corners. "An embarrassment to the family."

I gather the tossed containers. Everything I can think of to say is a trap. Either I'm a jerk for insulting his dead relatives or I'm a liar. I choose liar. "I'm sure he meant well."

"He would've been happy if the Sanford line had ended with him."

Francesca's telling me Leo's right, that Dr. Sanford was a monster. But I hear myself channeling Dr. Spangler. "He must've had some good traits." I peel open a container of cookies, homemade for me. I put one in my mouth and offer them to Leo.

"Of course," Leo says, taking a handful. "He was a great man." He wings a cookie toward his house. It turns in an elegant curve and disintegrates against a tree.

"And he raised you," I say.

"He loved to remind me how magnanimous he was to take me in, to care for the ne'er-do-well orphan when he had businesses to build and a town to take care of."

The mists are clearing; the world expands by degrees.

"But you were family."

"That made my shortcomings all the more grating to him. He was carrying out a plan that spanned generations."

Another cookie rips through the leaves. Birds chatter in the dripping treetops. The earth sighs as it drinks the rain.

"He worked his whole life for the town. But he didn't mind reminding me that I didn't have the stuff to carry on the Sanford destiny."

"What about your destiny?"

"All I ever wanted was to do one thing he'd say was worthy of the family name."

"I can't tell if you loved him or hated him."

"Neither can I."

A shiver ripples my shoulders.

The sky rumbles, distant and throaty. I notice the drone of the swollen river. I feel this moment imprinting on me, and I know I'll recall this someday, in the shadowy moments before sleep, or alone on a dark train, watching the moon.

"I wish I'd had the nerve to tell him he was wrong about me."

My brain surges in agreement. A plan forms, mine

or Francesca's, I can't know, but she urges me to take this opportunity. I put my face close to his and take his hands. "What if you could?"

Leo won't meet my eyes. "I imagined telling him a thousand times," he says. "Then he was gone."

I dare to take another small step. "What if he could hear you now?"

"I'd probably chicken out again." A breeze rustles the canopy, and water beats a gathering rhythm as it cascades from leaf to leaf.

I clasp my hands behind his neck and press myself against him. "What if I could help you?"

"I'd tell him what an ass he was." The words shudder out of his body. "I'd tell him I'm sorry for being such a screw-up."

"You're very special." My nails burrow through his hair to his scalp. My thumbs caress his clenched jaw. "He was a fool if he couldn't see it."

"He was a lot of things." Leo laughs like a boy who refuses to cry. "But he wasn't a fool."

"He was wrong about you."

"It doesn't matter," Leo says. "He's gone."

Steam wisps off the rooftops. A drop slides from my hair, runs icy down my neck. "I can help you." I can tell him the truth because it's unbelievable. "If you want," I push the words before I stop myself, "we could bring him back."

chapter fifteen

Our date ends too soon, but I make curfew, so that's a step in the right direction for my relationship with Grandma. My heart shrivels as Leo walks away, and I imagine that whatever is forming between us is being ripped out of me.

Alone upstairs, I gush romance into my journal along with rationalizations that my confidence means I'm ready for this relationship, even if my therapist might disagree. She probably wouldn't like my plan to invite Ezra Sanford into my head, much less my body, but I have to help Francesca. I try to ignore my anxiety and focus instead on the possibility that if he leaves behind his memories the way Francesca did, that I'll know the truth about his role in the murder of Mrs. Stirling.

Wind gusts through the room, and the rain resurges. My maple bends and topples to the floor, spilling a semi-circle of soil as it rolls.

I scoop the earth with my hands and replace it in the pot. Flecks of rain spatter the floor, and I wonder if Leo is getting soaked.

As I lie in bed, the wind and thunder roll like waves,

blurring into gray noise, rising and falling, luring me outside, across the wet sand to the pier where Mom waits with open arms. She's smiling at me, but also at Francesca, as if I've brought home a new friend, then she floats out over the pulsing sea, shrinking to nothing, and I awaken with tears in my eyes.

I dress in the dark and creep outside. Dawn is muted with fog. Birds dart among the gray-green branches. The trees luxuriate in the moist air. The earth seems to be in a prolonged exhalation. "*Before it's too late*," Francesca makes herself known. I wonder what happens when time runs out.

"I'm trying," I say aloud.

No one is around, but Francesca hears me. I don't know how I know it, and I think for an awful second that it's possible that I'm becoming her, that it's Francesca whose directing my thoughts, my body.

She's stirring things up. Between her demands and my own concerns, my thoughts flit like bees. I agonize over needs I don't understand much less know how to fulfill. But I have to find some way to control what's going on, do something I know I want to do. So, with the morning air cool in my lungs and damp on my skin, I set out to find Burt.

The sun must be up, but it's a soupy haze when I

reach the bridge leading to the village square. The river's monstrous from the rain, and the noise of it follows me.

Unlike everything else in this fairy-tale village, the bus depot is a dump. It's hidden away down a side street away from the square. Its glass doors are opaque with grime. One panel's held together by a forking strip of silver tape. Importantly, there's no police car waiting for the bus that rumbles out of the fog and hisses to a stop.

It's a great relief—from the fact that Burt's safe or that Leo told the truth—when the doors open and Burt steps out, greasy and carrying a small box draped in burlap. He sees me and stops. I wonder if he sees the guilt in my face.

"How was your trip?" I'm eyeing the box.

He runs his hand through his hair. "Didn't expect to see you." He smells like a barn.

The box rattles. "The mystery package?" I ask.

Burt lifts the cloth to reveal a cage. Inside, an animal jumps, a rabbit. Cedar chips tumble out.

"He's so cute," I kneel for a closer look. "Oooh, but he stinks."

"That jerk sent me all that way for a stupid rodent."

I shouldn't, but I find myself laughing.

"Yeah," Burt says, starting for home. "Hilarious."

"Wait," I say. "I have to tell you something."

Before I can begin to explain, Heather's jogging toward us in electric-blue spandex, graceful even when she's dripping sweat. She stops, not breathing particularly hard.

"You sure get around," she says.

I don't know if she's talking to Burt or me.

"Angel and I stopped by last night." She's talking to me. "To see if you wanted to go to the senior picnic."

"Sorry," I say. "That sounds like fun." I wonder if they hear my panic.

"Your grandmother said you were—"

"I just grabbed a bite in the square."

"Yeah." Heather becomes an accomplice. "Can't wait to hear all about it."

If Burt's reading anything into our conversation, he's not letting on. Heather squinches up her face. "What smells so wretched?"

"Long story," Burt says.

I lift the cloth again. "His new pet."

Heather touches the rabbit's nose, then looks up at Burt. "Please tell me you're not going to—"

"No," Burt says, but Heather's giving him a suspicious face.

"Why, then?"

"It's none of your business, really." Burt says.

"Everybody's keeping secrets these days." Her eyes flash to me.

"I'm going home," Burt starts to walk.

"Watch out," Heather tells me as she starts to run away. "Angel's on the warpath."

"Didn't take you long to get on Angel's bad side," Burt says.

"I don't know exactly what's going on with her." I say, hoping it's not what I think.

"You know she has a thing for Leo."

"That's what I wanted to tell you," I say. "I want to have another séance." He brightens. "With Leo." And he just shakes his head.

"What is it about him?" Burt won't look at me. "I've done everything you've ever asked. Stayed up all night looking for your ghost. Spent way too much on a crackpot fortune-teller. Broke into Leo's house."

We pass the cemetery. Shards of dew glimmer on the grass. Fog pools in the hollows.

I don't want to lie, and I don't want to hurt him. "Remember what Madame Zalenko said about spirits needing some connection to come back?"

"I got arrested for you."

"Leo has the best connections to Dr. Sanford."

"He's also rich and good-looking."

"He's an obvious link."

"I'm sure it's his uncle he wants to connect with." He opens the cemetery gate, sets the cage on the ground and opens it. The rabbit twitches its whiskers, takes a tentative step, and bolts into a bank of boxwoods. Burt dumps the cage into a garbage can.

"Leo's our best bet to help Francesca."

"Tell yourself whatever you need to."

"I don't know what else to do."

"Me neither." He says, walking away.

I follow him. I can't think of any way to convince him my plan is the right thing to do, so we walk in silence and finally we get to his house. I have to tell him.

"I'm going to Leo's house tonight."

"Of course you are."

"I'm doing this for Francesca."

"And it just so happens that you need to do it alone with Leo at his house."

"You're jealous?"

"I just thought we were getting to be … "

I shake my head. It hurts to hurt him.

"I've committed multiple felonies for you."

I resort to offense. "You did those things for you," I say. "So you could finally tell everyone you've seen a ghost."

"You're right. I did all that to see a ghost." Burt says. "But what if I hadn't convinced you it was a ghost, that you weren't losing your mind?"

He's right. If he hadn't insisted I was being haunted, I'd be alone in my room, wondering how long I could hide my hallucinations.

"Thanks," I say. "I appreciate it." I've lost my ability to sound sincere.

"I would've done that stuff anyway, probably."

"Anyway?"

"Even if you hadn't been so ... "

I cover my embarrassment with a laugh, and I wish the wind would carry away his words and me with them.

"So it's you and him?" he says.

"No," I say. "It's just me."

My grandparents are in bed at nine-thirty, and by ten I'm at Leo's house, in a set of rooms I've never seen. This area is comfortable and modern, with overstuffed chairs and a glass coffee table. A bar separates the sitting room from a stainless steel kitchen, and on the bar, a pair of candles flicker.

"Why are you wearing a tie?" I ask.

"For Uncle Ezra." His pride is endearing.

I wipe my palms, imagining the silk unknotting in my fingers, buttons sliding through holes. But I have a job to do. Despite his nervous cheeks glowing in the firelight, I have to maintain control.

"Besides," he says, "I thought you'd like it."

"Maybe you should take it off." I draw the curtains. "You should be comfortable for this."

"Absolutely."

"And the jacket," I slide the coffee table aside and sit in

the empty space, hands on my knees, palms up.

He sits opposite me, jacketless. "I must admit," his eyes hold me as he pries open his top button, "I'm a bit skeptical."

"Don't be." His twin shadows dance in giant tandem on the wall and ceiling.

"But promise me something," I say.

He holds up his hand to swear.

"What we're about to do does not leave this room." I scoot towards him, turn his hands palm-up atop mine. "Our secret."

Leo nods. "You, too, right?

"Not a living soul." I say.

"Then I'm a locked vault."

"Close your eyes."

"But then," he says, "I won't be able to see you."

His compliment takes the edge off my nerves, but I don't linger over it. "Do you know what you are going to say to him?"

"Yes."

His skin is electric. I take a deep breath and shake my hair to relax. "Say his name."

"Ezra Sanford."

Francesca growls in the back of my brain.

"Concentrate on him," I say. "Pretend he's here with us."

"You smell good," he says.

"Open your mind," I say. "Invite Ezra Sanford in. And be ready."

"Whoa. Did you feel that?" Leo pulls back his hands. "I actually got a chill."

"Good." I didn't feel anything. "Concentrate on Ezra Sanford."

Leo draws a deep breath and settles his hands back onto mine. "I'm concentrating."

"Say his name with me." I close my eyes and exhale, "Ezzzzzz-raaaaaaa."

Only my voice. I clear my throat and tap his palms with my fingers as I draw another breath. This time he chants with me: "Ezzzzz – raaaaaa."

After a few dozen repetitions, I feel nothing. My mind turns over the variables. Maybe my attic room has some special power. Maybe it only works with me and Francesca. Maybe I'm blocking him somehow, like I am secretly afraid to do this. Maybe Ezra doesn't want to return.

But I continue, concentrating on Ezra Sanford. Leo's hands twitch and go cold and soft like Mom's.

"Ezra?" I say. I open my eyes and Leo's sitting tombstone-straight, his eyes are open, but they're glassy. His face is bloodless.

"Ezra?" I repeat. Leo slumps onto his side.

"Leo?" I say. His eyelids flutter but don't blink. A forced, high-pitched wheeze, squeezes out of his throat.

I scan the corners for a phantasm.

"Mr. Sanford?" I edge closer.

Leo spasms, half choking and half wretching.

"What's wrong?" my voice cracks with fear.

He curls, bent like a fish, gasping. I grip his head to stop it flopping. His jaws are locked, and his eyes are wide and vacant. I'm thinking firemen and hospitals and should I run for the phone or try to clear his airway. His teeth grind with a sound like crunching gravel. And then they stop. He relaxes, his head limp in my lap, eyes open, lips quivering.

"Leo?" I say.

He makes two rapid blinks and his lungs inflate.

"Mr. Sanford?" I say.

His fists uncurl, and he closes his eyes. "*Doctor* Sanford," he says, his intonation awakens something deep in me, and my entire body resonates with despondent anger.

For an instant I pity Leo, wondering if he can see this. He must be feeling himself fade as Sanford's spirit takes hold. Then, *He still wants me dead* appears in my mind, and I shudder in the presence of some existential danger.

chapter sixteen

I'm twitching, revved up, ready to flee. But I force myself to be still. I look into his eyes and it's all I can do not to quail at the sparking, crackling man I've brought back to life.

"Dr. Sanford," I say. "Can you speak?"

Leo—his body, at least—sits up. He surveys the room as if witnessing something impossibly beautiful. "What is happening?" His baritone fills the room.

I inch away, partly in fear and partly to avoid the burning urge to attack the man, to unleash the anger that's been smoldering since before I was born.

He stretches his arms—Leo's arms—before him, turning them, working the fingers, wrists, elbows.

"Do you know where you are?" I ask.

He makes a lingering review of the rooms. "I recognize my own home," he says. "But who are you?"

"Do you remember how you got here?" I'm feeling my way behind the sofa, but I'm watching him, trying to seem casual as I distance myself.

Leo's body stands, taller somehow. He rubs his right hand in his left. "I was in the garden," he says. "It was an infarction." He blinks. "An inherited condition."

"I can explain." I can't though.

"The presentation was textbook." Sanford paces. "Ischemia resulting in extreme chest pain, sweating, sudden fatigue."

You deserved far worse bursts into my mind, but I keep it in.

"I collapsed in the roses. The pain was tremendous." He nudges open a curtain, spreads his fingers against the glass. "I don't remember recovering."

"We brought you back."

His forehead wrinkles at his—Leo's—reflection against the darkness. "Who?" he shakes head.

"Leo and I did."

He gives a skeptical laugh and turns on his heel. "Where is the mongrel?"

Dr. Sanford sees it's only me behind him, and he turns back to his reflection. He touches his cheek, gasps, and moans from deep in his chest as he falters.

He clutches my wrist for support, his chest heaving in terse spasms. I suffer his icy fingers and guide him to a chair. When he releases me, I rub the impressions of his fingers from my forearm.

"How can this be?" he asks.

The candles gutter, and our silhouettes shift over the walls, vanishing and reappearing in different shapes, different places.

"I'm dreaming." Sanford says.

"It's not a dream." I step into the kitchen, glad to have the bar between myself and him. "I don't know exactly how," I say, knowing he won't believe me, "but I'm afraid you're dead."

"Yet here I am, sitting in my parlor, in my house." His fingers play over the fabric on the chair. "I feel young."

"It's Leo's body."

He drums Leo's fingers. "But how?"

"I'll explain everything," I say, thinking *get him talking. Let him be the expert.* "We need your help."

He brightens with an expression so charming I think Leo has returned. "By all means," he says, but the voice isn't Leo. He crosses his legs, studying me. "But first, to whom do I have the pleasure of speaking?"

I want to hide. "Ingrid Van Hooten." I don't know what to do with my hands while he inspects me. "Has anyone ever told you, Miss Van Hooten, that your bone structure is exquisite?"

I cross my arms, touch my locket. Heat pours off my ears. "Thank you," is all I can get out.

"Clinically speaking, of course" he says, as if to defuse the impropriety of an old man perusing a young woman. "Fair, slender, Northern European, Dutch, from the name. But do I detect a Mediterranean breadth to the nose?"

I feel his gaze like spiders on my skin.

"Take no offense," he says. "I'm of the school that finds

diversification in breeding enhances a line."

My repulsion at being likened to livestock must show.

"Rest assured, you have exceptional features. And I detect a subtlety of intellect, which is, of course, the real prize."

His voice is commanding, authoritative, and coming from Leo's handsome face. The complete unreality of the moment leaves me dumb.

"We'd need the usual battery of screens, of course, but on first analysis, I'd say you're more than adequate."

I refuse to ponder what he is saying, but try to steer the conversation in the direction Francesca—and I—need.

"But I digress." He lifts his inquisitive brow. "How may I help?"

It is curious to feel so at ease with someone so despicable, but I seize the moment. "Do you remember Judge Stirling?" I ask. *Lead him to the subject.*

"I knew Leroy his whole life."

"Do you remember Mrs. Stirling?" The name churns my gut.

"Leroy's mother?"

"His wife."

Sanford's face betrays nothing. "Dorothy Stirling was a remarkable woman." Leo's blond hair shines in the candlelight.

"Do you remember how she died?" I stumble over the word in the presence of the dead.

"Yes." He stands, begins to meander. "But tell me ... " he looks directly at me, "how long have I been ... "

"Six months."

"Six months." He pronounces each word slowly, as if inspecting them for meaning. "No time at all."

"What do you remember about Mrs. Stirling?"

He makes a tiny, pensive sigh, almost a laugh. A smile crosses his face, then vanishes. "She was poisoned."

"You were her doctor. Did you try to save her?"

Sanford trails Leo's fingers over a table, picks up a framed photograph, sets it down. "There was nothing to be done." His mannerisms are so different I have to remind myself it's Leo's body. I wonder if Leo's here with us, and how I'll get him back.

"What happened?" I ask.

"Poor Leroy. He could scarcely believe the urchin could do such a thing."

"The urchin?" An old wound re-opens.

Sanford moves to the entrance to the kitchen. The bar that had been a barrier between us now pens me in.

"When she arrived at the Stirlings', she was eight years old. Not a day in school."

"Francesca, his maid?" I imagine scrambling over the bar.

"Yes. The Stirlings' housekeeper fished her out of some gutter in the city."

"Where were her parents?" I say. Francesca's telling

me this doesn't matter, but I'm intrigued with the fact that, despite having Francesca in my head, I don't know this.

"Her mother dumped her with some wretch she accused of being the sire, and disappeared. He died in prison, I presume."

"What happened to her mother?" I ask before I can stop myself.

He shrugs and waves a hand like he's dismissing a child. "You know how those people are."

The sensations come too rapidly to process: a filthy room, hideous men, hunger and the stench of human waste. Memories from another lifetime.

"Eventually the Stirlings managed to tame her." Sanford says.

It takes immense concentration to form words, to force them from my vocal cords. "And Francesca stayed on with Judge Stirling?" I know this, but I want him to tell me.

"He was fond of her," he says, "referred to her as a sister."

"Was there anything more between them?"

His sneer begs to be slapped. "She was his maid." He smothers the thought with disdain.

Sanford becomes distracted by his reflection—Leo's reflection—in the black glass of the oven door. I shudder as he traces the flawless skin around Leo's eyes.

I ease behind him out of the dead end of the kitchen. His eyes follow me in the reflection as I pass.

"But he let her stay," I say. "Even after she was accused

of murdering Mrs. Stirling."

"He was reluctant to believe it."

"He thought she was innocent?" I need him to confess.

"I told him about the poison. The police found the stuff in the tea she gave her."

"He believed her," I almost say "he believed me."

"He was convinced she'd be acquitted."

"Were there other suspects?" *Say it.*

"The girl admitted her guilt when she hanged herself."

His tone is terrifyingly convincing, like there's no capacity for guilt in the man. "There was another reason," I say.

"What, but her conscience, could drive her to take her own life?" Sanford says.

What was Mom guilty of? And even though I know I shouldn't, my anger takes over. "You know why she killed herself."

Sanford stares at me, impassive.

"Admit it." My hands quake with the desire to be away from Ezra Sanford, away from this house, this town, this life.

"This is upsetting for you." His voice is as quiet and emotionless as the burbling of a brook. "Let us not dwell on the past."

I grip the back of a chair, my head glowing with Francesca's rage and the rising tide of failure. This man won't give up his secrets. I won't save Francesca.

"I owe you a great debt," Sanford approaches.

"It's not me you owe," I can barely get the words out.

"You've given me a new life. Time to continue my work."

"No." My failure multiplies.

"You can't think I'd waste an opportunity like this."

"Leo," I cry. "Come back."

"A second chance, armed with experience."

"It's Leo's body!" I shout. "Get out!"

He opens his hands to me. "Don't," his voice is calm, like a man trying to corner a dog.

I edge into the portrait hall, walking backward trying to make it to the stairs. "Leo, where are you?" He backs me against the wall of portraits.

He snatches my wrists. "Stop!" I twist free. He lunges for me again but I swat his hand away. "Get out!"

"I'm not going anywhere," he says, blocking my blows.

I try to push past him, but he tosses me with the force of a wave.

My head hits the wall. My vision goes white as I crumple. A portrait crashes to the floor beside me. My face pulses with pain. I taste blood.

"Leo!" I try to shout, but it comes out a whimper.

"Leo's gone," Sanford stands over me, fists clenched, arm cocked.

I duck behind my arms. "Leo!" I scream again.

The blow never comes. Raising my head, I see Leo, shoulders slumped, making loose, erratic arm gestures.

"I'm sorry," his voice wavers, but it's his. "I'm sorry." He drops to his knees, but I skitter away. Pain drones in my ears, and I scramble down the stairs to the front door.

"Don't leave me."

I stop before I turn the knob. My tongue's metallic and swollen.

"What's happening?" he shouts.

I'm glimmering with adrenalin and terror. My teeth ring with pain.

Leo's looking at me like I'm the one who slammed him against the wall.

"I thought it would be me," I say.

"What are you talking about?"

"Your uncle was here."

Leo slumps against the wall.

Tears trickle down my cheeks, but I'm relieved that at least Leo is back. "I didn't get the chance to tell him."

"Tell him what?" Leo raises his voice.

"That's not true." I finger my jaw, tender from chin to ear. "I had the chance. I just didn't." It hurts to speak.

"Didn't what?"

My hand's still on the doorknob, and I want to run. "I didn't tell him how you felt about him."

"Oh, god," Leo slides down the wall. "I know exactly what he thought of me."

"I lied to you," I say.

"I know." He covers his face. "I remember it now."

"I should have told him."

"It feels like he's still here." His voice is fragile.

It occurs to me that he must have his uncle's memories lingering, the way Francesca is still in my head. "Give it some time to settle."

"He hated me." Leo's voice is fragile. He raises his hands and looks at me with bloodshot eyes. "And who is Dorothy Stirling?"

The question elates me, but I hate the look on Leo's face when he confirms his uncle's a murderer. My cheek is on fire, and though Leo's babbling, trying to talk through what just happened, I'm thinking about Dr. Sanford measuring the poison, mixing it into the tea, instructing Francesca in his cold physician's voice to brew it for Mrs. Stirling. I'm closing in on the truth, but Francesca still won't let me rest.

"We have to bring him back," I say.

"No." Leo said.

"We can get him to confess."

"He won't admit anything."

I knit my fingers together. "We have to try. We can record it." My suggestion is a high-water mark of my desperation. "Burt can help us get—"

"We're not telling anyone about this."

"I have to."

"I won't," Leo says. "Nobody can know."

"You'd let an innocent woman be branded a murderer for all eternity?" The words come out too harsh.

"I can't do that to them."

"Why are you defending him?"

Leo shook his head slowly. "It's not just him," he says. "My family." He's staring at something distant. "He was a great man," Leo said the words like he's repeating a litany.

"He was a murderer."

"Stop it!" Leo's shout echoes among the portraits. "I won't be the one who destroys the family name."

"What about Francesca Moss's good name?"

"She's nothing to me."

I've never wanted to strike someone so badly. "She's an innocent girl," I say. "She killed herself because of him. Your uncle killed a pregnant woman. His friend's wife. And he framed Francesca."

Leo huffs like an animal.

"Who would I be if I betrayed them?" His eyes range between pictures, his father, his mother, sideways on the floor.

"Would they want him to get away with murder?"

"Would they want generations of work ruined over one woman? Their legacy shattered?"

"What will their legacy be if you let this stand?"

"I have to protect them." "This is your chance to prove your uncle wrong. Prove that you're stronger than he is."

"I'll prove him wrong," he opens the door, "by protecting our family."

chapter seventeen

Madame Zalenko's curtains are drawn, but I can see light from inside. I'm clammy and my heart's in overdrive. I don't remember the walk from Leo's, only that it was dark and hot, and my mind won't let go of the horrible feeling that I've done something terrible to Leo and I don't know how to fix it. And I'm telling myself it wasn't anger in his voice as he ushered me out the door, but my face throbs from his—from his uncle's—blow. I don't want to be alone with all this, and I don't know what to do, so I knock again.

The youngish woman who lets me in—Madame Zalenko's roommate, I'm guessing—tells me to sit and wait. Her flowy top is unlaced pretty far, and her shorts show a lot of leg as she disappears down the hall. A grandfather clock strikes eleven. I should've gone home.

The chimes fade, and Madame Zalenko slinks in, her movements airy and muscular. Her lips are the color of lava. She holds a clear plastic bag. Her eyes hang on my violet cheek. "That boy do that to you?" Her words have all the time in the world.

"You said I should come back if I had questions." It

hurts to talk.

She moves to the table covered with liquor bottles and lowball glasses and a bucket, where she plucks ice cubes with silver tongs and drops them, one by one, into the bag. She wraps the ice pack in a cloth napkin, places it in my hands, and tells me to tell her what happened.

"I fell," I say, pressing the cold against my cheek.

"Don't lie to me."

The youngish woman in the flouncy top returns and slouches into a chair, takes up an emory board and goes to work on her nails.

"I need help," I say, "with the ghosts."

The long-legged woman looks up when I say this. Madame Zalenko notices me notice her and says, "Don't mind Suzanne."

"What makes them come and go?"

"I'll help you, honey, but you gotta be straight with me." She means my bashed face.

"It was ... " I can't say *Leo* and I won't say *Dr. Sanford*. "Someone else."

"You gonna see him again?"

"I have to."

"You need to take better care of yourself."

"You told me if I invite him, he might show up," I say, "But you said he might not leave."

"You told me you were inviting a girl."

"What happens if they ... " I can't believe what I'm

asking, "stay in your body?"

Madame Zalenko studies my eyes one at a time.

"Not me," I say, ashamed of what I've done to Leo.

"Somebody's in there." Her fingers are lotion-soft on my hand. She keeps staring, and I blush and try not to squirm. "You sure this isn't about your mother?" "Isn't" comes out "idden".

"It's Francesca, the woman I told you about. I need your help."

Suzanne's purposefully ignoring me.

"What *did* you do?"

"She took me." The words catch in my throat. This isn't what I came to talk about. But then I'm babbling. "I was floating away. I saw myself, but it wasn't me." Suzanne thinks I'm a flake. "It was like I was disappearing."

Madame Zalenko knows this already. She gives me an unhappy smile and pauses for a breath. "Close your eyes for a second," she says, "and imagine a chasm so deep you can't see the bottom." My mind sees the river, shrouded in fog.

"But you can see the other side, and it's close enough that a brave soul could gather up all her courage and strength and just maybe leap from one side to the other." Her cadence is rhythmic. "But after you make that leap, you'll be spent, and the longer you wait, the weaker and weaker you get. And if you try to cross back, you'll just fall and fall and fall in a graceful and doomed arc that will carry you closer and closer to the other side, but never there."

Half my face twitches, clueless.

"But every so often a bridge appears, a safe path across the chasm." My mind shows me the stone bridge by the cemetery, Grandma and me in her car, careening off the side. "And that's you." Madame Zalenko squeezes my hands. "You're the bridge."

I blink my eyes open. Madame Zalenko looks stern and kind.

"Your mother never told you about this?" she asks.

"My mother's dead."

She's not surprised. "You don't talk to her?"

"No." I'd rather jab the razor through my hand. "I invited someone else, too."

She makes a long blink.

"Can you teach me to control it?"

"Oh, sweetie, this isn't something you control." She sounds like Mom explaining puberty.

"I have to make him leave my friend."

"You got your friend possessed?"

"It's his uncle," I say. Francesca spews vicious thoughts at his mention. "And I'm afraid he'll come back."

"You're right about that," she says. "You're gonna have to help your friend get rid of him for good."

I know she's right. It's torture having Francesca in my head, constantly questioning whether my feelings are my own, whose thoughts are in my head. How much worse it must be for Leo, sharing headspace with a man who hates him, not to mention being a murderer. "How am I supposed to help him?"

"Start by asking," she says. "Polite but firm. If that doesn't work, you might have to get ugly."

I push for details, but she just tells me I have to make him—Dr. Sanford—uncomfortable. "You wanna get somebody outta your house," she says, "you gotta be strong."

"What do I do?"

I look to Suzanne for any glimpse of explanation. She stretches her long legs and gives me a "you asked for it" look. Her feet are bare, her toenails the color of tangerines.

"Trust yourself," Madame Zalenko says, and I look from Suzanne to her, and my head goes dead quiet, like something droning in the background suddenly stopped.

There's a knock at the door, and Suzanne gets up and checks a screen and says something that might be a foreign language.

"Set him up in the pool room," Madame Zalenko says. "Tell him I'll be a minute."

Suzanne lets in a man in a suit, but she gets him down the hall before I see his face, and I get the feeling she's blocking me from him, too. Something clicks: camera on the door, gentleman caller in the middle of the night. Madame Zalenko's not just a psychic, maybe she's not even a psychic. I'm considering everything she's told me in this new light, and all I can hear is her telling me to trust myself, and that's as good as it gets.

Madame Zalenko says I can stay if I want, but I can't risk giving the Witch that kind of ammo, so when Suzanne returns, Madame Zalenko tells her to drive me home, and they show me out through the kitchen and through a cloud of thyme and rosemary by the back door.

In the car, Suzanne tells I'm lucky to have Madame Zalenko helping me and she—Suzanne, that is, who looks about fifteen in the blue glow from the dashboard—drops me off at the house I tell her is mine.

I tap on Burt's window until he appears. His hair's defying gravity. I climb in and pace while he sits on his bed. Whispering with him in his dark bedroom feels dangerous, but the fog of dirty laundry makes sure there's not even a whiff of sexiness. I tell him about me and Leo and his uncle, and Burt just sits and listens with no expression.

Somewhere in the house a phone chirps.

I tell him how Zalenko said I have to help Leo get rid of his uncle, and that I have a plan, and I'm basically begging Burt to come with me. I'm feeling like Lucy holding the football for Charlie Brown, but I feel like I owe him, and, if I'm honest, I'm afraid to go alone.

He agrees to come with me, but only if I let him bring his camera. Before I can protest, Burt's bedroom door opens and both of his parents are gaping at us, and guess whose grandmother just called looking for her.

chapter eighteen

At breakfast, Grandma tells me to pack up, and I think she's sending me back to the Witch. It's been awkward since Grandpa picked me up at Burt's house last night, but I hadn't sensed this level of frustration. They raised their eyebrows at my "tripped over a broken sidewalk" version of why my face is purple, but they didn't come out and call me a liar. I get the impression that they're as concerned about my health as they are flummoxed by my actions. My inability to explain isn't helping. It stings to think they're giving up on me.

"We're not sending you back to the city," Grandpa says. "We're all going to the Peach Tree Inn. It's just down the road." He explains that we're moving out so the construction crew can speed up the renovation.

Francesca's telling me I have to stay, I have to stop the demolition. The more we remove of the old house, the thinner her connection to this world becomes.

"On the bright side," Grandpa says, "they'll finish off your room."

"Finish off my room." My chest tightens at the words.

I'm a little girl, reading on the floor of my room—the attic room—while a woman who isn't my mother but who feels motherly sews by a dim lamp.

"It'll only take a few days."

The B&B is beautiful and generic, and I fear this is what my grandparents' house will be when they're done: stripped of the past until it's as clean and lifeless as a dry sponge. I feel like something's being taken from me, like I'm being erased. Francesca's imploring me to please please hurry and I can't turn her off, but I can't help her, so I just sit on the sterile porch of the Peach Tree Inn and simmer.

My grandparents would be justified in thinking I'm everything they feared: a liar, a delinquent or just plain crazy. I had one stupid paper to finish to get back into school, and I barely scratched out an outline. My head's too jammed to focus. Maybe medication is the answer. Maybe this is just a figment of my imagination. Maybe the drugs will turn it off.

I'm imagining a conversation where I tell Burt I'm going to ask Dr. Spangler to find me some nice, quiet clinic where I can rest. Just thinking of that conversation makes it real enough to possibly be true. Entertaining the prospect of surrender feels good. But I tell myself it's too easy. Then there's a voice I recognize but it takes me a second to process that it's real.

"You're a hard girl to track down." Mr. MacLeish is cheery. Behind him, a pair of burly guys strain to lift a large bonsaied pine from a truck.

"Is here okay?" Mr. MacLeish points to the end of the driveway. The tree is from Leo's garden. One of the tree-bearers sucks air and grunts, and the tree wobbles.

The guys set the tree down and heave for breath.

Mr. MacLeish hands me a clipboard with a delivery receipt.

"Why did you bring me a tree?"

The historian rips a form from the clipboard. "Gift from Leo Sanford."

I stare at the receipt. The pen shakes in my hand.

"He made a lot of gifts yesterday," Mr. MacLeish says. "Wanted to settle some things before he left."

"Left?" I say. "When?" This is my fault.

"He brought his lawyers to my office yesterday," says Mr. MacLeish. "Made out a new will. Arranged a number of things to take care of in his absence."

"Where'd he go?"

"I was hoping maybe you'd know," Mr. MacLeish says.

I don't know anything—where, why, anything. What I do know is that giving away possessions is a big red flag. It occurs to me that Mom didn't even leave a note. I wonder if his uncle's making him do this, and I'm hating myself for starting this. Tears blur my vision, and I lower my face to the tree. The soil is chunky and dry in my fingers.

"Needs water," I say.

"Precisely what his instructions say," Mr. MacLeish hands me a binder. "I guess he chose the right caretaker."

Grandma and Grandpa come to see what's going on. Grandpa looks at the bonsai and whistles through his teeth.

I push my finger into the soil to test the moisture.

"Which leads me to the second reason I'm here," says Mr. MacLeish.

Under the surface, my finger touches something smooth and cold.

"Leo gave some records to the WHS. A bunch of papers that belonged to his uncle. He told me that you might be interested in some of them."

My fingers close around the object, and from the loose soil I remove a key.

"Ingrid?" Grandpa says. "Did you hear Mr. MacLeish?"

The key is a heavy, forged relic. I cover it with my hand and look from Grandpa to Mr. MacLeish. I slide it into my pocket unnoticed. "Excuse me?"

"I suggested," says Mr. MacLeish, "that you might like to come by to take a look at some of the papers Leo sent to the WHS." When I respond with a stare, he adds, "Perhaps they're relevant to the history project you and Mr. Giles were working on?"

Something's happening. I don't know what, but I won't figure it out if I stay here. So I look to Grandpa. "Can I go now?"

The ledgers and files from Sanford House fill the WHS with a fresh must of flaking leather and dust. Mr. MacLeish calls out to someone as we enter, and Burt calls back from somewhere within the stacked boxes. My heart flutters from broken to fused with a speed that makes me nervous. But I accept that I am truly glad to see him, and I'm worried that I can't show him how good this makes me feel, because it's not him I want.

"I stayed up half the night with this trove," Mr. MacLeish fondles a stack of papers on a work table. "I could hardly tear myself away."

"What is all this?" I ask.

"They say in this life we see only the back of the rug." Mr. MacLeish is quiet, like he's talking to himself as he turns pages in a cloth-bound ledger. "The tied knots, the loose threads, the bare outline of the pattern."

Burt gives me a look like he's proud to be elbow deep in whatever this is, excited that we'll find something to help Francesca, to help me. But this is Leo's doing. He brought these things for me. And then he left. And I never got to fix him, or even to thank him.

Burt sneezes into the crook of his elbow.

Mr. MacLeish is still talking, "supposedly, in the world to come, if there be such a thing, we get to see the face of the rug in all its glory, to see the pattern God has woven through our lives."

Burt smiles like he's humoring Mr. MacLeish.

"Occasionally, though, we get to peek at the front of the rug a little early." Mr. MacLeish turns a brittle page. "And it turns out God wasn't the only one doing the weaving. Looks like the Sanfords had their fingers in the loom, too."

"What's in there?" I ask.

"A very interesting portrait," he says with the zeal of a historian getting first crack at a primary source. "Of an exceptional, and exceptionally philanthropic, founding family."

"Are you going to tell me or what?" I ask. Mr. MacLeish looks at me over his glasses, and I try to smooth my harsh tone. "I mean, this is interesting."

"These records date to the origins of Warwick," he says. "The original Sanford granted a hundred-twenty-seven thousand acres for the village and the preserve around it." Mr. MacLeish says. "The town charter is full of lofty talk of creating a modern utopia, of their *noblesse oblige* to craft an ideal town for the people of Warwick." Mr. MacLeish is pleased at our attention. "They were modest to a fault. No grand monuments, just quiet prosperity." MacLeish says.

"But luckily for me they kept immaculate records."

Mr. MacLeish explains how the Sanfords' charity grew less anonymous over the generations, so that by the time Leo's parents drowned, the family's patronage was renowned. "Now, Burt," MacLeish says, "we're getting to information directly on point to what you were asking about the other day."

Burt flushes, and he looks like someone's ruined his surprise.

"Dr. Sanford, when he was running the municipal show, was inclined to return to an era of secrecy, but not out of modesty."

Burt's looking over Mr. MacLeish's shoulder.

"Your suspicion," MacLeish says to Burt, "that the good doctor had some unsavory means of getting things done was prescient."

It chafes me that Burt's taking credit for spotting Dr. Sanford's villainy, but I want to hear more.

"From what I've pieced together so far, Dr. Sanford adhered to an 'ends justify the means' kind of philosophy. He manipulated council votes, did some tricky things with elections, and by the time he became mayor, he had his hands on just about every lever of power in the village, twisting arms and extorting favors to further the family plans."

"I knew he was corrupt," Burt announces.

"Not your garden variety greed, though." MacLeish

goes on to explain that many Sanford projects actually cost the family a great deal of money.

I test the rusty hinge of my jaw as I listen, opening and closing slowly, locating the point of maximum pain to distract myself from the thought of Dr. Sanford's altruism.

"It's going to take some research to root out all Dr. Sanford's machinations," Mr. MacLeish says. "But whatever shape he was hoping to grow his ideal village into, he wasn't afraid to prune some branches along the way."

MacLeish tells us about someone called Hasbrouk, who refused to sell some land for the hospital expansion. "Two weeks later the perfectly healthy patriarch died. His family demanded a medical examination, which concluded the cause of death was 'undetermined natural causes.'"

"Let me guess," Burt's foot is tapping. "Dr. Sanford did the autopsy."

Mr. MacLeish nods.

"This is more than fishy, right?" Burt asks.

"It's not for an historian to judge, necessarily," MacLeish says.

I wonder how much of this Leo knows. I wonder if Dr. Sanford communicates to Leo the way Francesca communicates with me. If so, I'm guessing he's angry that Leo's exposing all this.

"What do you make of this?" Burt thumbing through a ledger.

I recognized the format from Grandpa's farm records.

"It's a stud book."

Burt does his one-eyebrow thing. Even Mr. MacLeish seemed puzzled.

"Like a family tree," I say, "but for a herd of livestock."

It's impossible to tell what bloodlines the book traces because instead of names, the book tracks pairings and births by nine-digit numbers.

I turn to the index, where the numbers are cross-referenced with names. What I read chills me to the root. These aren't animals; they're the people of Warwick.

"That's Angel," Burt says. He checks the book and page numbers indicated beside Angel's nine-digit number and shuffles through the pile for the corresponding ledger.

"Give me that," I remove the book from Burt.

The information compiled on the townspeople is dreadful: medical histories, criminal records, charitable contributions, business associations. My stomach sours, and my throat burns.

The stud book has exacting analyses of potential marriages, and where preferred unions occurred and bore offspring. That's the word the book uses for babies.

Mr. MacLeish points out that the lengthy, clinical discussions are written in Dr. Sanford's own handwriting. He leans back in his chair, removes his glasses and rubs the bridge of his nose between his thumb and index finger. "Dynastic marriages meets eugenics?" MacLeish theorizes.

"Selective breeding for humans?" I offer.

"This can't be legal," Burt says.

Mr. MacLeish makes a noncommittal face and returns his glasses to his eyes. I scan pages, excited to be closing in on proof that Dr. Sanford's as ruthless as Francesca believes, and far more bizarre. I'm scouring columns for the nine-digit number corresponding to Francesca Moss when another entry catches my eye: Dorothy Gardiner Stirling and a blank for her unnamed child. Where the child's number should have been, there's only the notation "terminated in utero." I'm flooded with memories of terror and grief and hatred. Francesca's screaming inside me.

The line linking Mrs. Stirling to her child spurs from a number different than Judge Stirling's. This number rings familiar, and I'm certain it was the patient number on the paternity test that Leo torched on the mountain. All I have to do is find the name that corresponds with the father of Mrs. Stirling's child. The fact that it's not Judge Stirling means someone had a motive to poison Mrs. Stirling. My joy is magnified by Francesca singing in my head. I turn the pages till I come to the heading, "S."

The Sanford lines thread throughout the books, and my circulatory system's chugging with adrenalin as I follow the Stirling family tree closer and closer to the final generations. I locate Leo's grandfather, but when I turn the page, nothing makes sense. There's no mention of Leo's parents, nothing about Leo, and nothing about Dr. Sanford.

"There's a page missing," Burt touches the torn remnants

in the crease of the book. Hope evaporates.

Burt walks me most of the way home, but he's not keen to face my grandparents after last night. So we part ways a block from the B&B. Francesca's buzzing in my subconscious, but it's a happy buzz for a change. I've placated her somehow, and it's only after I start walking not north but west, turning the key in my hands, that I realize I'm going to Sanford House. I'm sure the key has something to do with something at his house, but with Leo gone, I have no idea what I'm even looking for. I should've shown the key to Burt, should have brought him with me. But Francesca doesn't care about any of this. She's telling me to keep going, to find what Leo wants me to find, that time's running out.

I ask myself, or maybe Francesca, how I'm supposed to get inside Sanford House. And even if I find something that will help Francesca, how am I going to summon Mr. Stirling? How will I make him believe the truth? And if I ever see Leo again—the thought that he's gone hits me like a hammer—how am I supposed to exorcise Dr. Sanford? Francesca just keeps repeating Madame Zalenko's advice, and sometimes I think it's really Dr. Spangler, and other times I imagine it's Mom, and sometimes it's all of them saying: *trust yourself.*

But every window at Sanford House is lit. Shadows

move behind the curtains. Leo hasn't left town after all.

I ring the bell.

Something smashes inside.

The front door's unlocked, and I shout for Leo. A metallic crash echoes out from the clinic. I follow the noise through the hallway littered with papers. Another crash draws me to the records room. A metal filing shelf leans at a dangerous angle against another stack, both on the verge of collapse.

I call for Leo again.

"It's about time." The answer comes from inside the room, but it's strangely muffled.

"Where are you?"

"In here."

I follow his voice, slipping over the papers to the back of the room. A cabinet has been pushed from the wall to reveal a thick door open into a windowless room. Inside, rows of ledgers line the walls. Leo steps out, an open volume in his hands.

"What are you doing?" I ask.

"Waiting for you." My chest seizes at his rich, bitter baritone.

"Dr. Sanford?" I ask, but I know it's him.

"Who else have you told?"

I step back. The toppled shelf groans metallically. Files slide and fall to the floor. My hand moves to Burt's recorder in my pocket.

"Speak!" Sanford-in-Leo hurls the ledger. It flutters past my head and clangs into the shelf beside me, its spine crackling as it flaps to the floor.

"I haven't told anyone." I'm backing away, watching his eyes as my hand, behind me, slides the recorder switch to "on". He follows, matching my retreat step for step.

"Liar." He lunges.

I recoil, but his fingers close around my wrist.

"Leo, come back!" I scream and twist, but I can't break his grip. He clamps onto my other wrist and yanks me off my feet. Pain explodes in my shoulders. "Where are you?" I shout, wondering if Leo hears me.

"What did he tell you?" He squeezes both my wrists into one hand while his free hand unbuckles his belt and whips it from the loops.

"You're hurting me!" I flail, but he wrenches my arms, spinning me to the floor. He kneels onto my chest, and his weight flattens my lungs.

"Leo!" Starved of air, my scream fails.

Leather coils around my wrists. "Shut up," he says, cinching the belt until my bones grind together. He binds me to a metal shelf.

I gasp as he steps off me. "Leo," I yell through my tears, high and piercing this time. "Come back!"

Sanford stalks out of the file room, his footsteps squeaking away down the hall.

I scream for Burt, hoping the recorder is transmitting.

I try to work my wrists, but the belt holds firm. Sweat blurs my eyes. I gasp, hyperventilating, suffocated by fear. My skin's ablaze, but for the cool strand of silver around my neck, and my locket, pressing like ice against my sternum. I contort my torso and stretch against the belt, twisting until I can reach my chain. My fingers spider along it until they close on the locket. My thumbnail separates the halves, and the blade, brittle and sharp, falls into my palm. Heaving for breath, trying to glean oxygen from the dead air, I pinch the razor between finger and thumb and saw at the belt.

The door slams open, and Dr. Sanford glowers into the room. His visage darkens Leo's face, and he swings a metal can.

Sanford opens the cap, and the can thunks as a sweet, caustic vapor permeates the air. He sloshes fluid over the piles of paper, and the poisonous stench takes me back to the garage with Mom.

Hefting the can in awkward arcs, he douses walls, floor and shelves as he makes his way to the vault hidden in the back wall.

The vapor stings my eyes. I can barely feel my fingers as I slide the razor again, nibbling at the stiff leather. My sinuses burn. Colorless spots swarm before me. "Leo?" I choke. "Are you here?"

"Yell all you want," Sanford emerges from the vault and chucks the empty can. It hits the wall with a hollow clunk. "Leo's not coming back."

"I know you killed her." The sound came from my mouth, but they're Francesca's words.

"Which is why you can't leave," Sanford says.

I'm shouting for Burt and for Leo and to please please please hurry, but my stomach turns and I choke as bile sours my mouth.

The razor slips from my fingers. I lunge for the glinting blade, but the belt jolts me to a halt. I hang all my weight on the belt, ignoring the shrieking pain in my shoulders and wrists as I strain to sever the remaining leather. The metal shelves creak and shift, but the belt holds firm. "Leo," I whimper. "Please."

"He was always weak," Sanford pats my head as I struggle lamely against the belt. "And to think I trusted all this to that pusillanimous ingrate." His feet squish through the noxious puddles back out in the hallway. "And he just wants to hand it all over to people like you."

Again, I hang every ounce of me against the leather. The cabinet groans and topples toward me. I try to roll out of the way, but I'm bound to the collapsing shelves. I duck as best I can as the top shelf crashes against the wall, screeching as it bends under its own weight. The metal whines as it settles. I pull again. Rivets pop and the shelf separates from the frame. The belt slides free, and I roll, wrists still tied, out from under the shelves as they snap and slam to the spot I just vacated. The razor gleams on the floor ahead of me.

I lay in the wreckage. Sanford rattles a box of matches.

"Why?" I croak.

"I hate loose ends." Leo's broad shoulders blur against the fluorescent glow from the corridor. "And I don't need you interfering now that I have this young, fresh body to work with."

A match snaps, and the air ignites with blinding orange heat. Fire blooms from the carpet and swirls up the walls. Smoke pools along the ceiling. I push myself onto my elbows and knees, coughing as my bound hands sweep the floor until they land on the razor. I struggle to lift the smooth blade from the floor when he grabs my arms and drags me upward, pinning me from behind. "But before I leave," he hisses into my ear, "I need you to return that key." His arms wrap me tight.

"I don't know what you're talking about." I kick and thrash, but he drags me deeper into the incinerator that was the file room.

"Don't think I don't know what Leo's trying to do," I strain against him as he paws at my pants. "Where's the key?" he shouts. He finds the digital recorder, drops it to the floor and crushes it beneath his heel.

Flames roar as they feast on the papers. I arch my spine and drive the back of my head into Sanford's face. He grunts with pain, but his grip loosens, and I flail free. He snatches at me and knocks me to the floor. He hauls me back up again, but I come up with the razor and swipe. Steel meets flesh, and the blade carves a red valley across the back of

Sanford's hand.

He howls, blood gulping from the gash, and releases me. I slouch, gagging, into the foyer.Every breath scalds my throat. I pull at the front door, but my blood-wet hands slip from the knob. A cry freezes me.

"What's happening?" It's Leo. Quiet, confused, sad.

"Leo?" I call into the smoke, choking and limping toward his voice. He's doubled over in the file room door, wrapping himself around his sliced hand, blood streaming through his fingers and down his legs.

"Leo?"

His eyes brim with despair. "I'm sorry." His words barely cross the din. "He's too strong." Then he dashes into the flames.

"No!" I shout, as I follow him into the inferno.

"Run!" He shouts, stumbling further into the blaze. Smoke roils almost to the floor, gushes into the hallway. Every inhalation chokes me with hot poison. "Come with me," he shouts in Dr. Sanford's vile voice.

Leo staggers into the vault, black clouds swirling around him. "Get out!" Leo shouts.

"No!"

"Please!" Leo screams at me. "Go!" Then his face goes calm. "Remember me," he says. He forces a smile and pushes the vault door closed. The locking wheel spins. In the distance, sirens wail.

I swear I hear his voice as I drag myself to the front

door. He is calm and clear through the chaos, telling me to save myself. I stumble out into the night air and collapse. The world swirls blue and red, chilling my arms, feet, hands, spine. Each inhalation is agony. I choke and cough on the ashy lawn while Sanford House burns with Leo.

chapter nineteen

The ambulance ride's a masked blur, and the antiseptic emergency room barrages me with flashbacks to the last time I spent the night in a hospital. But this time I'm the patient. A cannula oxygenates me while gloved nurses draw blood samples until my levels come into line. This takes way too long, but this time, at least, the patient gets to go home.

By home I mean the Peach Tree Inn, where I'm confined to the property. I sit on the porch where a deep overhang shades me from the midday sun. Part of me gloats with Francesca's cruel pleasure at the end of Ezra Sanford, but most of me is smothering under the guilt of Leo. I see him closing the vault door, saying goodbye, apologizing for I don't know what. But I know how he feels. In a flash he returns and vanishes.

Francesca continues to needle, but she's weaker now. Sanford's demise brings her some joy but no relief, and every time she speaks she's further away. If it's not too late already, it will be soon. I worry that if she disappears, she'll take part of me with her.

The worst part of having Francesca with me is knowing

she's innocent, but not knowing how to make anyone else believe me. Sitting on the sunny porch, I try to pull Mr. Stirling into my mind. Even if he makes his presence known, I have no idea what to say to him other than tell him the insane truth and hope he believes me. Francesca's desperation is mine, and when I close my eyes I see her drifting in an oarless boat, water trickling in.

Heather strolls into the yard, red-eyed and sallow. It's a pleasant surprise that she's come to check on me, but it turns out she's looking for Angel. Nobody's seen her for two days. When I ask if that includes her parents, she looks at me like I'm a moron. Even so, I feel about a hundred times better having Heather here. She says that Angel never talks to her parents. She thinks I already know this, that Angel has been a nomad for a while. When I ask where Angel lives, if not with her parents, she says it doesn't matter, and I feel even worse about how I've treated Angel.

Neither of us knows what to say about Leo. When we try to talk about him, we just mumble stupid platitudes and end up crying. I'm trying not to collapse into a black hole-type emotional vortex or spin apart into bits. Leo's dead. And if it weren't for me, he'd be alive. She wants me to help find Angel, and I get the feeling that she would settle for any company at this moment. And I'd like the company, too, and I'm worried about Angel, but between Francesca and Leo, I don't really have the bandwidth for another problem. I tell her it's not a good time for me to be asking permission to go anywhere, and though I feel lousy for doing it, I ask her to pass along a message to Burt.

Heather gets the message to Burt, and when I reach his back yard that night, he's ready. Heather is there, too. She's too sad to be alone, she says, and I understand so completely I don't even have to respond. I show him the key and he recognizes it immediately, and in taciturn unison, we three start for the cemetery.

The sky is sinking low. The moon finds a hole in the clouds, paints the world dirty gray, then fades again. Fireflies blink and dissolve, promising a pattern that refuses to materialize.

If I'd shown the key to Burt first, I think, Leo might be alive.

The frogs and crickets cover our footsteps. We're almost to the cemetery gate when we find Leo's car, abandoned in the grass.

In the cemetery, I sense the dead winking like the stars behind the clouds, and I hear them in the rattling breeze. The air glows with their humid distillations caught between their decaying bodies and whatever lies beyond.

The pyramid cuts a triangle from the sky, unnaturally straight, looming larger with every step. The force of Burt inserting the key moves the door, and we stiffen as it swings open, smooth and silent as ice.

Cold radiates from inside. I feel fear like a needle against my neck. From the darkness of the pyramid comes a voice, feeble but dulcet. The singing sounds like it's miles away, but I recognize this tremulous contralto.

Burt hears it, too, and clicks on his flashlight. The song stops cold, and Angel's startled scream puckers my skin. She scurries in the dark. Burt's light flashes over stone, the wall of crypts, a leg. A glass bottle clatters across the stone floor.

My heart crashes against my sternum. Dr. Sanford's voice rasps in the back of my head, his icy nails clamp my wrist, and I brush my arms to dispel the illusion of his clutch.

Burt freezes Angel in his light. "You scared the pus out of me."

"Thank god," Heather says, running to her.

A dreadful calm settles over me. The inward-sloping walls converge high beyond the flashlight's glow, and on the opposite wall stand rows of doors numbered with the dead.

Angel shields her eyes from the flashlight. "You mind?"

Burt lowers the flashlight, and the room glows gray from the reflection off the stones. "What are you doing here?"

"Saying goodbye," Angel drones. Heather hangs on her

arm.

"You're a mess," Burt says.

"Oh, Burt." She devotes a full second of vocal fry to each syllable.

"We should take you home," I say before I can stop myself.

"You torched it," she sings. "Remember?"

I'm about to deny this when the barb catches.

"You were living with Leo?" I ask.

"Jealous?" Angel's laugh is humorless.

Jealousy's one of many feelings as I leap to my own defense. "You said there was nothing between ... " But the truth clunks into place: The GALS embargo was a lie; Leo kept our date a secret; Angel pushed me toward Burt to keep me away from Leo. I feel stupid, angry, betrayed. But I'm the interloper. I've lied, too. And because of me, Leo's dead. I can only guess what's keeping Angel from exploding.

"It was nothing for a while," Angel shrugs. Her legs give, and Heather helps her to the ground. "At first."

Burt sniffs the bottle and sets it upright on the floor.

"Just him being a gentleman," she says with a flourish, "rescuing me."

I'm reeling with sympathy and guilt and the itching sensation that we aren't alone.

"And then it *was* something—" her voice vibrates with sadness. The corners of her mouth turn up, and her eyes pale. "And then it was nothing again."

Burt scans the wall of crypt doors.

"I had no idea," I whisper, wondering if I would have acted differently if I had known.

"I don't care," Angel closes her eyes. Her words ring as true and as sad as anything I've ever heard.

"I'm sorry."

"Least I got his car." Angel flops onto her side, her head on Heather's lap.

I look at Burt, the key cold in my hand. Burt's standing by the crypt marked for Leo's body. I imagine his corpse in a morgue drawer. He wants me to do this. So I open the crypt door. Fear skitters down my spine as I reach into the dark hole.

Angel gurgles something up, swallows it back down.

Shoulder deep in Leo's crypt, I half expect Dr. Sanford's cruel fingers to seize my wrist and to haul me inside. In real life my fingers touch paper, and I remove a pair of envelopes. One bears my name in Leo's messy script. The other reads "Angel".

I hold the envelopes to my face, searching for his clean, soapy smell, his peppermint breath, and I ache with his absence. My envelope contains two folded pages.

The paternity test is on top, the one we stole from Mrs. Stirling's medical file.

Angel burbles wetly.

"That sneaky bastard," Burt's looking over my shoulder.

It feels good to hear him say it, as if Leo's with us. We

can joke with him; we don't have to speak of him in hushed tones. For a second I think of Burt as a bridge.

The second rag-edged sheet is the missing index page from the stud book. Circled in red is the name Ezra Stirling beside the same nine-digit number on the paternity test.

I feel my feet lifting off the floor. "We have to do another séance," I say.

"Are you sure that's a good idea?" Burt says.

"Guys!" Heather shouts.

Angel retches. Her skin's gone a bilious yellow, and her stomach's convulsing. A bubble forms on her lips and pops.

"Angel!" Burt's pries her mouth open, turning her head.

"Wake up!" Heather's voice cracks.

"The hospital," I say. "Do you see the car keys?"

Heather fumbles through Angel's pockets. "Got 'em," she says.

I'm stuffing the envelopes into my pocket and trying to stay calm. Burt and I hoist Angel between us, and her feet leave twin trails as we drag her to Leo's car.

chapter twenty

Angel's limp and ghastly in the fluorescent emergency room. At the sight of the pale, barely lucid girl, she's on a stretcher and we're banging through doors. We leave out the fact of her camping out in a mausoleum. I'm crushed with the fear that this, too, is my fault, that I'm doomed to relive this scene, that anyone near me risks becoming trapped in my vicious loop. I've fallen through a crack in the universe, dragging everyone around me through this moment over and over until I can fix it.

It's midnight when a doctor announces that Angel's stable. They're keeping her overnight, and they chase us out. I hope that I'll get to deliver the envelope in my pocket. But, in the meantime, there is one thing I can maybe fix.

Burt resists, but I convince him to take me to my grandparents' house. My third floor bedroom is empty and quiet as the bottom of the sea. All that remains of the furniture are rubbed spots where the feet have marred the wood. The sill is naked without my maple, and the emptiness brings a pang of loss. But it still smells of mice, and I hope there's enough of the house left for Francesca to return.

Burt's flashlight shines on the dusty rafter that was her gallows.

"I still think this is a bad idea," Burt whispers though there's only me to hear.

"You're the one who wanted to see a ghost."

"What about what you said happened to Leo—"

"What I *said* happened happened."

"So what if it happens to me."

"You think Stirling's as evil as Ezra Sanford?"

"But if you summon him, and he doesn't leave ... "

"I promised Francesca," I say, and I regret what I'm asking him to do, but I ask again.

"You really think you can just make him appear?"

"I don't think I can make anyone do anything." My hope is that between Burt's friendship and the fact that we're in his house, we'll have enough of a connection to Mr. Stirling. "But I can invite him."

I lay the paternity test and the index page on the floor and sit down. My motions are deliberate; I'm stretching time to focus my thoughts. Burt and I sit facing one another like the other night. I take slow, deep breaths and call Francesca, and almost instantly she's back in my head. The chain around my neck becomes a rope, and my hands and feet go numb. Decades of loneliness and rejection settle onto me, and I feel myself detach, my senses let go, and I move beyond them.

My eyes are closed, but I see Burt sitting before me, arrested by my change. My body wobbles slightly as it inhales, exhales, my arms relax, and my hands slide off my knees. I slump sideways.

"Wait," Burt says.

But I don't wait. I keep calling Francesca, soundlessly, and as I watch from the cold pinnacle of the empty attic room, I no longer see myself, but Francesca on the floor below.

Burt watches in horrified silence as my body sits up again. My eyes open. I find myself in easy communication with her, sharing thoughts, and we both know that Francesca now possesses the truth she's been seeking.

"Tell her it was Doctor Stirling's baby," Burt says to my body.

"I know," my mouth replies with Francesca's voice. Vindication blossoms with the relief of finding a truth affirmed, the reassurance that I, that she, might finally be washed clean.

"Ingrid?" Burt raises his hand, and I feel warm spots on my arm.

"After all these years." Tears flow from Francesca, following the dry curve of blood around her chin, pooling in the black bruise against the noose. "It's comforting to know I haven't been lying to myself." Her black lips curl upward. "But I need to show him. Leroy needs to hear this truth."

Burt's flashlight goes out.

Fresh blood streams from my nose, and my skin glows chalky, shimmering from a light from no possible source. The air around Burt glimmers, and his skin takes on a translucent shine. A new figure, a man, resolves over him, and I gulp down the urge to stop this from happening. But my fear evaporates at the man's voice.

"So many times I felt your presence." Judge Stirling's voice trembles with low, sad strains. "Thinking you were Dorothy, cursing you for taking her from me."

"Dr. Sanford would have killed you if I told." Francesca says. Her fear rolls through me, but I tell Francesca we're safe. I'm sad, but at peace.

"I was blind," Stirling says.

"My life was over." Francesca says. "It was the only way I could save you."

Stirling takes Francesca in his arms. I flush at the contact, embarrassed to share these sensations. Their embrace continues in an unreal stillness, a connection not corporeal but spiritual, their energies communing through me.

I feel Burt's energy, too, and it's awkward but pleasant, some new or forgotten variant of love, not skin-tingling arousal but a fundamental relief, satisfying and rejuvenating. The sensations fill me like warm water, and they tease my comprehension with images, thoughts, sensations swirling around a sense of reunion. I don't know where, but I sense the rebirth of an intimacy so complete that the self is no longer distinct from the other.

I can't say how much time passes until I stir. I awaken on the floor, my head on my outstretched arm. Something warm touches my wrist, and I look up to see Burt gaping as if I've sprouted wings.

"We did it." A smile takes over my face. "They ... " I stop at his blank stare. Burt shakes his head slowly.

"How long was I ... " I don't know the word for what I'm asking.

"I feel, like," Burt says, "hollow."

"Francesca's free. He knows the truth." Uncountable seconds pass. "Did you see them?"

"I don't remember anything."

I feel sorry for him, for not having the experience. "I couldn't have done it without you."

"I did absolutely nothing."

I make him look at me to hear this. "You believed me."

The next morning I'm surprised when Grandma's tone sounds almost like her disappointment in me is waning. This particular disappointment stems from her belief that after she let me go to the WHS, Burt and I snuck back to the old house. I can only imagine what she thinks we were doing there, but I let her believe it because the truth just might get me sent off to an asylum. And, apparently, it's within some acceptable range of transgressions, because she almost seems willing to have forgotten about it as we drink our coffee.

The surprises continue when Heather and Angel show up, and that they're talking to me is a miracle. Seeing Angel, I realize how deeply afraid I was that I might not see her again. Now here she is, sprawled across the porch swing like she's just finished a good yoga session. She looks tired, but her color's back and she's in good spirits. I think about giving her the envelope. But I can't bring myself to bring it up just yet.

"They pumped me full of fluids," she says, "and drained about a gallon of blood, but they say I'm normal. Sort of."

"And she's never," Heather says with wet eyes, "ever, ever going to disappear like that again."

"Like you could stop me." Tough Angel's back.

Heather's arms vine around Angel. "Do you know what you put me through?"

"You've only mentioned it about—"

"I can't lose you, too." We're all crying now. "I can't lose another friend."

"Where will you stay?" I ask, wondering how long it will be before I can ask any favors of Grandma, even one for someone else.

Heather looks away, and I wish I hadn't asked.

"I'll figure something out," she says. "Six months till I'm eighteen."

For someone whose boyfriend just died, whose been abandoned by her parents, whose few possessions just went up in smoke, she's putting on a brave face.

"You'll stay with me," Heather says, "I'm sure I can convince Mom, given the circumstances."

"I'll be on my best behavior," Angel says. "I'm a changed woman."

"Ordinarily," Heather says to me, "I'd be calling bullshit." A line of mascara hangs from Heather's eye, and I'm baffled at why they're both hiding grins. "But Angel's about to explain why I believe her this time."

"I guess I have a new-found respect for life." Angel brushes a tear from her cheek.

Neither of them will make eye contact with me, and for a strange moment, I feel like Leo's here. Heather blots her eyes with the hem of her shirt.

Angel goes on. "Remember all Leo's complaints about," here her voice goes deep, "'it's so hard being the last Sanford, it's up to me to uphold the family traditions'?"

I imagine Angel's words and our collective memory might give Leo something to coalesce around, like rain precipitating out of fog.

"Don't make fun of him." Heather sounds genuinely offended.

"My point," Angel says, "is that it wasn't true."

Angel straightens her spine and flutters her lashes. Something's changed among us. Nervous drops form on her forehead. She lays her hands on her stomach.

"Are you ... " My mouth hangs open. My eyes fix on Angel's belly.

"'Tis true," Angel smiles.

"I still can't believe it." Heather covers her mouth. Her voice modulates between terror and pity and maybe joy. Angel's face is hot pink, and, entangled in Heather's embrace, she looks at me with pleasant embarrassment.

"Are you okay? Is everything okay?" I'm babbling, bouncing in my seat. "Who else knows? What are you going to do?"

"I'm fine," Angel said. "Everything's fine. I mean, everything's a fucking mess, pardon my French. But healthwise, it's all good." She's grinning and tears roll unabated over her flushed cheeks. "I have absolutely no fucking clue what I'm going to do."

My thoughts kaleidoscope. I'm terrified for Angel, not to mention how impressed I am that she's holding herself together. Mostly, though, I'm shuddering at the idea of what would I do in her position.

"Well," Heather says what I'm thinking, "we support you no matter what."

"I'd like to keep this between us girls," Angel says. "For now at least."

Heather's shaking with tears and laughter.

My emotions are swirling; envy, anger, and jealousy all tell me that if I could stop this then Leo will be mine after all. But he isn't mine. He never was. Leo belongs to Angel now, forever.

chapter twenty-one

It's standing room only at Leo's funeral. The mayor insisted the event bear the pomp and circumstance due the Last Member of Warwick's Founding Family. The existence of the unborn Sanford remains, for now, a secret between three women and a handful of medical types.

Heather, Angel, Burt and I loiter in the back and try our best to keep it together, but still one of us cracks and then we all crack. The pain comes and goes. Sometimes it squeezes the oxygen right out of my blood. But the waves are spreading out, losing intensity, and this triggers a deeper sadness, because it reminds me he's really gone.

The mayor and some other men I don't know talk for way too long. It's nice to hear them talking about all the good things the Sanfords did over the years, but it's clear that none of these men knew Leo at all. They're eulogizing the family more than him. I get a little sick every time one of the speakers—and every single one of them does this—pays homage to the Great Man that was Doctor Ezra Sanford. *At least Mr. MacLeish knows the truth,* I tell myself. *And hopefully he'll write that book about it.*

As the service is finally breaking up, word gets around that the kids are getting together at the pit later, and even Grandma understands that I have to go. So I guess she's coming around to me actually being normal. Just to drive the point home, or for maybe some other reason, I spend what's left of the afternoon finishing my history paper. It's not exactly the world's finest, but I can't just blow it off. My old teachers and headmistress didn't have to give me a second chance. I want them to know I appreciate it, that I didn't, you know, just take the easy way out. Why it matters I don't know, but I want them to know I'm taking care of myself.

It's dusk when Heather and Angel and I walk to the pit. I have Leo's letter to Angel in my pocket, thinking that this would be a good place for her to read it. When we get there and see all these guys milling around with tight faces and downcast eyes, though, I realize she should read it in private. I shouldn't have held onto the letter for so long, and every minute I keep it, it gets harder to imagine giving it to her. I don't want to let go of this piece of him.

There's a crowd of people I don't recognize but who all know Angel and Heather. There seems to be some unspoken rule that we're only supposed to talk about Leo even though nobody knows what to say. It's not like the official funeral at all, where it seemed like all the grownups were trying to out-mourn each other. Instead it's like nobody's sure how to act, but it's strangely honest. I feel like I'm the experienced one in this situation, but I feel phony because I'm guessing all of these guys knew Leo a lot longer and a lot better than I did.

Heather and Angel are talking with a girl I don't know, and I excuse myself to look for Burt. It doesn't feel right to introduce myself to anyone, so I just wander among the clusters feeling out of place.

Toby's prying apart a pallet and feeding the wood into the fire. He has it stoked dangerously high. With so much drinking going on, I should be running for home, but for whatever reason it isn't bothering me. It's funny how much I miss Dr. Spangler, how much my imaginary conversations with her fill these spaces in my head.

Jeff's in a tree, sitting on a branch about ten feet off the ground, leaning against the trunk and staring. He sees me notice him and nods but doesn't speak. I wave back and keep circling the fire, and soon I'm back to Toby. He's holding the long, iron poker like a harpoon, stabbing the fire over and other. The flames must be fifteen feet high, and I'm afraid the burning pile's going to avalanche onto us. It's so hot I feel like my hair's going to ignite, and when Jeff turns to me and I see the dry tracks, I realize why he's sticking so close to the flames. He jams the poker into the ground and opens two beers and holds one out for me. I can't not take it.

"To Leo," he says and takes a swig.

"To Leo," I echo, and the words catch in my throat. I drown my sob in a deep swallow then pour the rest into the fire, the hot rocks hissing and spitting as the beer evaporates.

"One for you, bro," Toby says as he dumps his beer after mine. I'm caught off guard when he puts his free arm around me, but I lay my head on his shoulder and just shake as I cry. My eyes are closed, and the world is orange and hot, and I can tell by Jeff's sniffling that he's crying, too. I just stand there in the heat and the glow, Toby's shoulder shaking against my cheek, the smell of smoke.

Toby goes on for longer than I expect before he settles down and takes his arm off me. "It's okay," I say, regretting the platitude as soon as it's out.

"Dude," he says, "This is a lot of things, but none of them is okay." The act of speaking cracks him again, and he closes his eyes and stifles another outburst.

"You're right," I say, and I hug him with both arms. I'm glad to be comforting someone else for a change. "But it will be." We stay like that for a minute, then I hear Burt just before he bangs me on the arm.

"Hey," he offers me a pipe.

"I don't think my therapist would approve." I say, and Burt turns red and starts apologizing so much that I have to hug him just to make it stop. Then he's crying, too, and I start again, and then I'm laughing about how if I don't stop bawling I'm going to dehydrate and Burt lets go of our hug and takes my hand and pulls me through the crowd. People stare as he leads me to a bunch of coolers and digs down into the ice and fishes out a bottle of water and unscrews the cap and hands it to me. The cold is divine against my hot cheeks, and when I put it to my lips it's the most refreshing thing I've tasted in my life.

"Leave some for me." It's Angel.

"You want me to get you a beer?" Burt says.

"I'm good." She takes my water with a smile and gulps it down.

If anyone has the right to be sad, it's Angel. She's in an odd place because even though people knew she and Leo had been together on and off, they have no clue what she's really lost. But now she's sitting on the same log where she was when I met her, laughing and crying at the same time, keeping her secret. I admire the way she's playing this, not milking her condition for attention. Or maybe she's embarrassed or ashamed. I'd be terrified, probably hide in my room or run away until it was over. Of course, it'll never be over for Angel now, or for Leo.

An hour or so passes. The fire's died down to normal, and the crowd's left. Jeff's sitting in a folding chair, staring at the sky with his hands tangled in his curls. Toby squats by the fire, leaning on the poker. Burt, Angel, Heather and me sit on the ground with our backs against the fallen log, watching the flames.

"What do you think Leo'd think of this?" Angel asks.

"This wouldn't be this, if he were here," Heather says.

"You think he'd want us to be moping around."

"I do," Burt says. "I think he'd love that we're all sitting around talking about him."

"Probably true," Angel says. "But what if it was one of us?"

"It was one of us," Toby says in a voice like lead.

Angel looks to Toby. "If you died, do you think Leo'd let us all hang around like sad sacks?"

"What do you want to do, play kickball?" Jeff says.

"Let's go for a swim." Angel suggests.

The silence makes me feel sorry for Angel. "I'm in," I say.

"Fine," says Heather. The boys join. And without another word we slip down the bluff to the water. Angel's not shy about stripping down to her bra and panties, and I overcome my hesitation by telling myself that this is exactly what Mom would have done. I haven't had a nightmare about her in the longest time since it happened, and as strange as it is, I miss seeing her, even like that. So I undress, too, thankful for the darkness as we wade into the pool.

All I can think of is the last time we were here, and how different things are, and how different everything is forever. I float on my back with my eyes closed, listening to the pebbles clicking in the current and the muffled rippling of my friends as my tears merge with the stream, flowing to the sea to mingle with Mom's ashes, and I see us swimming, doing silly leaps off the pier, her laughter louder than the birds and the wind and the waves.

Nobody says a word, but it feels good to be together.

We climb the muddy bank to bask in the warmth of the fire, and we dress and douse the embers and walk back to the village in the dark. The guys peel off, one by one, until it's just me and Heather and Angel, and we're taking a long time to say goodbye at the edge of Heather's driveway, and I finally tell Angel I have something for her. She recognizes his handwriting on the envelope and it's a long moment before any of us can talk again, and I want to see what's inside so badly, to hear his words, but we share one more hug for the night, and I walk home alone.

chapter twenty-two

We moved back to the house, and there's not a hint of mouse in my room any more. Francesca's gone, too. I miss Mom more than ever, now that she's gone from my nightmares. Last night, as I was drifting off, I called Leo's name in long, whispered breaths. But when he came it was only a dream. His eyes shimmered silver, and his hair was the color of snow.I was brimming with questions I couldn't form. His smile was jagged lightning, and I burned for him. The thing I most wanted to ask him, though, was if he'd seen Angel.

The light is just now seeping over the horizon, and the cemetery glows cool and beautiful. My bag sways in time with my steps, and for some reason I'm thinking of the papers Leo signed before he died. He gave away a lot of money and stuff, wrote a will, set out instructions for his funeral. It's hard not to imagine him writing the will as some kind of self-fulfilling prophecy, but, in my heart, I believe he made those arrangements to protect himself from death, not to invite it. His first instruction was this: no dark mausoleum for Leo. So he lies in the earth, his grave outside in the sun and the rain.

Eighteen months ago, Dad and I stood on the pier. Arrows of sunlight grazed the shoreline. The wind sang, and a curtain of rain hung between us and the horizon.

"Let's get this over with." Dad managed sentiment with his customary efficiency, and he upended the urn. The bigger chunks plopped into the waves; the rest of her mounted the wind, a gray swarm glittering through the stray light, my last glimpse of Mom.

I sit beside Leo's grave with my legs folded beneath me. "Thank you," I say, and "I'm sorry." I scrape a handful of dirt from the mound and sprinkle it back down, searching for his scent. I water his grave with tears.

Mom's ashes melded with the sea and the sky.

"Would you like to say something?" Dad asked.

I bit back my rage.

"I'll see you inside," he said. I pinned my hands under my elbows to keep them from the blade in my locket. The measured clop of his wingtips diminished to nothing.

I wanted to dive in, to swim until I was spent, too far to drift ashore, way out where I could float in the gray waves between the living and the dead.

Drained of tears, I lay on my back beside Leo. Great oaks wave against the sky. I fix him in my mind, his ice-blue eyes, his fine golden hair, and the grim sparkle of satisfaction as he sealed his uncle in the vault. I tell him how I'm swimming again, and how I've decided to stay in Warwick, about my music and Grandpa's garden. I talk about our dead mothers and living alone, and of babies and boys and men, and I etch promises into my bones.

From my bag, I remove my maple seedling, heavy with bright leaves, every node swollen with the future. I remove a trowel and the photograph I found my first night in the attic, freed from its shattered frame.

One day I'll look back and wonder if this could possibly have happened. Will I recognize the handwriting in my journal; will I believe the words? Time will alter my memory, and I wonder which details will be the first to fade, what I've forgotten already, what I failed to notice. Will I still believe in ghosts? Mom's gone. Leo is gone.

I stab the trowel into the earth at Leo's feet. I contemplate my new school, my new friends, how I'm letting my roots grow out. I ease the maple from its pot and place it into the hole.

When the roots are covered and watered, I take the photo of Mom and Dad and me. I imagine Mom's reaction to my decision to repeat her life, to live with Grandma and Grandpa. I tell her I want a life like hers. I tell her that she may have taken herself out of the world, but not out of me. I open my locket and remove the razor.

I will give Mom a second chance. I will hold her thoughts in my head, see the world through her eyes, just as now, in the rising light, I see my own eyes reflected in the glossy photo.

I press the blade in a smooth arc under her chin. I remove her from the photograph and slide her into the silver frame opposite the picture of me, cannonballing off the pier, and I close the locket against my chest.

acknowledgments

Ingrid, Burt and Francesca came into being as a thousand-word story inspired by a prompt from my friend (and years later, publisher) and shaped by our amazing instructor and mentor. Growing that story into this novel took help from a lot of good people, and I'm pleased to thank Joni Albrecht and David Robbins for their invaluable efforts from start to finish. Thanks, too, to my other writing instructors along the way: Ms. LaFevre, my kindergarten and first-grade teacher at East Harper Elementary, who made me write a story every day, Ms. Jaffee, who introduced me to journaling, Jaime Feuglein, whose praise and critique fueled my return to writing, Anne Westrick, Becky Bikowski, and the late David Jenkins at Willliam & Mary. And bless those poor readers who suffered through so many drafts, but improved every one: Bo Bowden, Lenore Gay, Dusty Hooke, Dave Hooke, Amber Hooke, Ellen Brown, Jules Hucke, Ann Wick, Cal Wick, Mig Dugdale, and especially Erica Orloff. Thanks to Wendy Daniel and Lynda Hatcher, who polished the story and gave it shape. Thanks to everyone at

James River Writers for creating a community of artists in Richmond, Virginia. I'm lucky to have been carried by so many guides, mentors, friends, and family, especially Belin, Henry and Catherine, but this novel would never have been possible without Alletta, my inspiration.

CPSIA information can be obtained
at www.ICGtesting.com
Printed in the USA
FSHW020752210820
73172FS